"What's this 'for the rest of our lives' business?" Holly asked.

Colin handed Holly a hot dog in exchange for one of the water bottles, hoping she didn't decide to hit him with hers five seconds from now. "Didn't I tell you? Well, I guess there is just one more thing you're probably going to bring up from time to time over the years, so maybe I should have mentioned it sooner. You see, I've given it some thought, and I've decided that I'm going to marry you."

Okay, Colin acknowledged to himself as he pounded on Holly's back until she could breathe again, so there were *two* things he probably should have said to her sooner. One, he was going to marry her and two "Maybe you shouldn't take a bite out of that hot dog until I tell you number one."

KASEY MICHAELS

is a *New York Times* and *USA TODAY* bestselling author of more than sixty books. She has won a Romance Writers of America RITA® Award and a *Romantic Times BOOKclub* Career Achievement Award for her historical romances set in the Regency era; she also writes contemporary romances for Silhouette and Harlequin Books.

KASEY MICHAELS

Bachelor on the Prowl

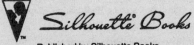

Published by Silhouette Books

America's Publisher of Contemporary Romance

To Tara Hughes Gavin,
so she has a matched set.
Okay, Mike, to you too…

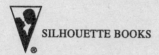 SILHOUETTE BOOKS
®

ISBN-13: 978-0-373-47092-1
ISBN-10:   0-373-47092-4

BACHELOR ON THE PROWL

Visit Silhouette Books at www.eHarlequin.com

Printed in U.S.A.

Chapter One

Every woman has a fantasy. Some wish for a handsome prince to come riding up on his white charger and carry her away to that legendarily well-touted Happily Ever After. Some long for fame on stage or screen, being the one woman in the world every man sees, desires, goes majorly stupid over. Some long to be captains of industry, and can actually see themselves in snazzy corner offices, wielding their power with a brilliance that earns them the cover of Time *magazine.*

Holly Hollis had set her sights a little lower this fall day in New York City.

All she wanted—and only for an hour, at that—was a man. Living, breathing, capable of walking and chewing gum at the same time.

Just give her a man.

Ah, come on, somebody send her a man.

Oh, and could some kind providence please make him a size thirty-eight long…?

Fifteen minutes earlier...

"Jackie! Brides *glide.* They do not *clomp.* Maybe you're modeling Eddie Bauer Mountain Momma wear next week, but this week it's *Sutherland's,* and Sutherland designs call for gliding. Got that?"

"I can't help it, Holly. It's these shoes. They're too small." Jackie, the six-foot-tall model, her bones and skin—she may have had a fat cell sometime in her life, but she'd banished it long ago—made a face. She was clad in a Sutherland bridal gown, looked fabulous, but walked toward Holly Hollis like a duck in hip boots.

"Shoes!" Holly called out to anyone who'd listen, and within moments there were a half-dozen hands holding out a half-dozen pair of shoes. White satin pumps. Ivory lace-covered heels. Plain shoes. Shoes with silver buckles. Shoes with heels so curved they looked as if they'd warped.

"Size? Come on, come on. Concentrate, Jackie. What size shoe do you wear?" Holly commanded, and Jackie told her. Holly smiled. There is a God, and She gives small pleasures when She can. "Okay, somebody find me a size twelve for Jackie."

"Gosh, Holly," Irene Collier said, frowning. "I don't think we have any twelves. Twelves? Couldn't she just wear the boxes?"

Think, think. Holly had to think. "Okay, look," she said to Jackie, tipping her head back to glare up into the model's eyes. "Tell me what shoes you wore here today. Maybe they'll work."

Jackie frowned. Not a lot, because she was twenty-eight now, and the thought of frown lines were one of her obsessions. "Hiking boots. Brown lace-ups."

Holly pursed her lips, sort of swung them back and forth over her teeth as she searched her left brain, then her right brain, hoping for inspiration. "Nope. Some designers would put hiking boots with a wedding gown and call it a new look. But not Sutherland. Okay, here's the deal. Barefoot, Jackie. You're going down that runway barefoot."

Jackie raised one well-waxed eyebrow. "You're kidding, right?"

"Wrong," Holly said, taking the model by the elbow and guiding her over to the short set of steps that led up to the curtain behind the runway. "You're a blushing bride. On the beach in Maui. At dawn. Irene—tell her escort to get rid of his shoes. And his socks! Don't forget his socks. Then tell him to go down the runway first, stand at the end, holding his arms out for Jackie's entrance."

"At the end of the runway? Barefoot? You sure?"

"Don't push, Irene. I'm working on the edge here. Okay, Jackie. You carry your flowers—Irene, flowers! That's it. Now, Jackie, you carry your flowers in one hand, use your other hand to sort of lift the front of the gown as you trip along the beach to your intended. Not clomp, not jog, not even trot. You *dance* across the sand, love in your eyes, your heart pounding, your veil caught in the ocean breeze. Feel it, Jackie. Feel the morning sun on your face. Smell the salt air. Irene, give me tear-jerker romance music. Something with swells in it or something like that, okay?"

Jackie had her eyes closed, "feeling" the scene.

Jackie was a "method" model, whatever the hell that was. Something like a "method" actor, Holly supposed, except she got paid better, and the hours weren't so long. "I see it," Jackie said. "Yes, I see it."

"Well, whoop-de-do, she sees it," Holly muttered as Jackie went tripping off to Maui—or down the runway set up in the main ballroom of the Waldorf-Astoria hotel. "Size twelve? The woman could stomp out small villages. Okay, Irene, what's next?"

"You are overworked, aren't you? That's it, Holly. Jackie was the last before the grand finale, and that's all set, already running like clockwork. We've got a good crew, one person assigned to each model. Take a break, maybe even breathe. We've got fifteen minutes before the last bride goes down the runway and you have to go out there."

Irene handed Holly a clipboard, then went in search of a flower girl model who she'd just seen—in her lovely white gown—ripping open a chocolate bar.

Holly staggered over to the refreshment table, snagging a can of diet soda before finding an empty chair and collapsing into it. This was her first showing without her boss and friend, Julia Sutherland Rafferty, by her side, and if she ever had to do another one without Julia's help she'd have to first go heavily into self-medication.

Holly had come to work with Julia when Sutherland was little more than a dream. They'd set up shop in Allentown, Pennsylvania, Julia concentrating on ready-to-wear clothes for the young and young at heart. Washable, affordable, cut on simple yet classic lines—perfect for the young mother, the female executive, the increasingly fashion-conscious grandmother set.

In other words, Julia's designs had a universal appeal, and the small Allentown business grew in leaps and bounds, until Julia's designs were shown twice yearly in New York, just like all the other "big" designers.

Holly hadn't known a gusset from an inseam when she'd started out with Julia, as her area of expertise had been in crunching numbers, chasing after overdue orders, hiring and firing—the nuts and bolts sort of work that left Julia free to create.

But the creative end of the business called to Holly, and she'd studied everything she could get her hands on, watched Julia, and soaked up knowledge like a sponge. Now, more and more, there were other employees to do the books, the ordering, the payroll and such, and Holly had taken over more of the "outward" part of the business.

Meeting with buyers, broadening their customer base, even sitting in with Julia as she selected materials, having some input on new designs.

The whole experience had been a joy, from the first day she and Julia had opened the door at Sutherland to today, when the company had grown to be one of the most recognized brands in the country.

Julia and Holly had become much more than simply employer and employee. They'd become friends, close friends, which was why Holly had been so thoroughly shocked two years earlier when this Greek god of a guy had shown up and introduced himself as Julia's husband.

Holly took a sip of soda. Man, that had been a day.

That had been weeks of "man, what a day," actually, until Julia and Max Rafferty had figured out that their separation had been a mistake and Holly got to watch a little "happily ever after" up close.

Julia's dad and mom, who'd been unhappily retired in Florida, had happily moved back to Allentown, and now Jim Sutherland oversaw much of the actual production while Julia and Max—and now Max, II—lived in Manhattan almost exclusively, near Max's businesses.

Julia relied heavily on Holly, and Holly liked that, liked the responsibility, enjoyed the pressure.

But she hadn't counted on being in charge of the initial showing of Julia's new interest, bridal wear. Sure, she'd always attended all Sutherland showings, but it had been Julia who'd run them, and run herself ragged, taking care of any last-minute glitches, herding models, pinning ripped hems and taking the applause and bows at the end.

But Julia had Max II now, and she left her five-month-old only rarely. She *had* planned to leave him with a sitter today, but Max had the sniffles, and Julia had dumped the entire show in Holly's lap saying, "I know you can do it."

Holly looked around at the chaos that circled her like a gaggle of dyspeptic buzzards. Models, everywhere. Gowns, everywhere. Makeup artists, seamstresses, caterers, little kids chasing each other, male models posing as if there must be cameras hidden everywhere.

And yet she'd made it to the homestretch with only one glitch—Jackie's big feet. Thank God Jackie was only scheduled to model two gowns.

Holly longed to slip into the crowd of reporters, buyers and society matrons on the other side of the curtain, just for one quick minute, to hear how they liked the show so far. She could still do that, as she wasn't Julia; tall, beautiful, definitely recognizable Julia Sutherland Rafferty.

Because she was just plain old Holly Hollis. All five feet one inch, and one hundred and six pounds of her. Nobody noticed her, never did, not in this fashion world of the giants. She could slip outside, listen to the buzz and know whether or not the latest Sutherland venture was looking like a hit or a miss.

Holly put down the soda can and got to her feet. She walked over to the makeup area and peered into one of the mirrors, checking to make sure she didn't look as wild-eyed as she felt. Nope, still the same old Holly Hollis.

Her chestnut hair always looked out of place, because it had been cut to look that way. Short, spiky on top to give her some needed height, with wisps cut into the sides and at the back, then sort of combed forward, to touch on her forehead, her cheeks, her nape.

Julia had talked her into the cut, saying that her small frame cried out for a little drama, and that the cut accentuated Holly's huge green eyes, set off her slightly pointy chin.

"Right," Holly said now to her reflection. "Now all I need is a harness and a sky hook, and I can play Peter Pan on Broadway."

"Um…Holly?"

Holly turned around, to see Irene making a face. Not good. Irene didn't make faces. She endured. She conjured miracles. She followed Holly around with a figurative broom, sweeping up problems and making them disappear.

"Problem?" Holly asked, figuring that, at the least, the Waldorf had just caught fire.

"It's the finale," Irene said, wincing as she took the clipboard from Holly. "We're minus the groom."

Holly looked around the huge room, counted heads. There were male models all over the place. "What do you mean, we're minus the groom? Pick one."

"That won't work, Holly," Irene told her with the tone of someone pointing out that, yes, by gum, the sky *is* blue.

"It won't work?" Holly asked, abandoning her idea to go scope out the reporters and buyers. Oh well, she probably wasn't dressed for the part of Secret Squirrel anyway, not in her kelly-green sheath, her wrist pincushion and the pink feather boa she'd forgotten she had wrapped around her neck—an expensive accessory for the bridal lingerie portion of the showing she didn't want stuffed in some sticky-fingered model's purse and walked out the door. "Don't tell me it won't work, Irene. I don't want to hear that it won't work." She sighed, then ended, "Okay, tell me why it won't work."

"Here's the logistics," Irene told her. Irene loved to use the word logistics. She liked other words, too, like *extrapolate,* and phrases like *in conjunction with.* At forty-seven, her stay-at-home-mom years behind her, Irene had decided to forgo going back to teaching and had looked for a "glamour job." Only she couldn't quite beat the teacher part of her into submission all the time.

"Don't say logistics, Irene," Holly begged, rubbing a hand over her forehead. "My head hurts when you say logistics. And if you're standing there trying to figure out a way of slipping *in my considered opinion* into your next sentence, I warn you, I may just have to hurt you."

Irene was tall. Julia was tall. The models were all tall. The whole world was tall. And Holly sometimes got tired of looking at everyone's kneecaps. It could make her moody.

"Don't pout," Irene said, obviously deciding that today was a moody day. "Now, I'll explain. As you know, the finale is a parade of eleven of our bridal gowns, each model being escorted down the runway by a groom. That leaves the big moment for Jackie to enter wearing Julia's real showpiece, the peach *peau de soie*. Eleven plus one, for a total of twelve. Thirteen's unlucky, remember? But Jackie has to have a groom, and we only have eleven male models. A tall groom, because Jackie's…well, she's tall."

"You're all tall," Holly grumbled. "The world is prejudiced toward tall people."

"You mean, the world is prejudiced against small people," Irene, always punctilious, corrected.

"I mean I'm *short*," Holly said hotly. "Look at these gowns. I tried one on, you know, just in case my mother's prayers are ever answered and I actually need some silk and lace. And I *drowned*. I looked like a little kid playing dress-up. First thing I'm going to do when this is over and I see Julia, is to tell her that there has to be a petite collection. Not just smaller sizes, but designs that won't overpower us short people. I mean, the gown I tried on had the loveliest poof sleeves. And I ended up looking like Joan Crawford in one of those thirties movies. Shoulders out to here,'' she said, using her hands to show the width of her shoulders. "I could play fullback in my nephew's peewee football league.''

Throughout this tirade, Irene had been counting male heads, watching the door, and counting heads again. "You're through?" she asked with the patience of a mother of five. "Good. Now, back to our problem.''

"No problem,'' Holly said. "We just ax one of the other bridal gowns and slip the groom on Jackie's arm.''

"No can do,'' Irene said, holding out the clipboard to Holly once more. "This is the finale, Holly. CNN is here, filming the whole thing for their special on weddings. One by one—with escort—we send eleven fantastic gowns down that runway, not twelve, because Jackie can't wear two gowns. Each gown with its own close-up and description. That's mega airtime for our ladies. Which one do you want to ax, and then wait for the hysterics? We got these top models because we promised them CNN, Holly. Do you want to take a chance on losing any one of them for Julia's next showing?''

Holly glared at her assistant. "I hate it when you're right.''

"Ten minutes, Holly,'' Irene said, glancing at the silver watch on her wrist. "What do we do?''

"Can't she walk alone? What's the problem with her walking alone?''

Irene rolled her eyes. "Are you forgetting that gown? It's the show gown, Holly, not really meant to ever be worn by any halfway *human* person. I think the thing weighs seventy pounds, and that's without the head-piece. Jackie needs an arm to lean on, or she's going to end up facedown in the front row of laps. That would look real great on CNN, wouldn't it? And I don't think Julia wants today's event to appear on some television blooper show.''

Several thoughts went flying through Holly's brain, most of them painful, and none of her ideas workable. ''Find out who this model is who was a no-show. I've always wanted to be able to say *you'll never work in this town again.* When I find him, that's what I'm going to tell him. I'm going to tattoo it on his perfect fore-head.''

''Nine minutes,'' Irene said, continuing her count-down.

Holly came to a decision. ''We yank the eleven male models and pick one to escort Jackie.''

''Airtime, Holly. For the boys as well as the girls. You'd have a riot on your hands, and I hate to see handsome grown men cry. Besides, the first two brides have already hit the runway—with escorts. Oh—eight minutes and forty-five seconds, Holly.''

''Trying for a second career doing countdowns at NASA, Irene?'' Holly bit out, then grinned. ''Yes! Irene, look over there. At the door. I think I see our man. Quick, what's his name?''

''Well, better late than never, I suppose,'' Irene said, consulting the clipboard once more. ''Harry Hampshire. Has to be a made-up name, right? Sic him, Holly, while I get the tuxedo ready. And, please, don't give him that you'll never work in this town again line until *after* the finale.''

Holly was already halfway to the door. Harry Hampshire, huh? He didn't look like a Harry. He looked, actually, like some sort of Greek god. Max Rafferty looked like a Greek god. Harry made her second Greek god in two years. That had to be her quota. She doubted she would see another in her lifetime.

Tall, definitely tall enough to make Jackie look fragile, he had the slim, muscular build of the professional model. A mane of blackest black hair, one lock sort of slipping down onto his forehead. Blue eyes that sparkled inside a fringe of black lashes any woman would die for. Full lips that were more sensual than hot fudge licked from a spoon. That square, model jaw, those creases in his cheeks as he returned the smile of one of the female models.

Dear God, he made Holly's palms itch. Gorgeous on a stick. Masculinity refined, smoothed, and yet definitely not domesticated. The kind of guy who'd actually look good in a morning beard. The kind of guy who smiled and that smile made you blink, because surely this guy couldn't be human. No human could be that perfect.

Yeah, well, so much for waxing poetic over some skin and bones.

"You're late, buster," Holly accused, grabbing his arm as he winked at one of the models. "Come on, we've got like seven minutes to get you into your tux."

"I beg your pardon?" the hunk said, although he did move along with her, which was a good thing because Holly was more than ready to try tossing him over her shoulder and personally stuffing him into the tux.

"Look, Harry, I've got no time for this. Strut on your

own time, okay? We've got—Irene! How much time have we got?''

"Six minutes," Irene called out, lining up more of the other models, each of whom had her own attendant with her, ready to fluff out the train on each gown before the model stepped on the runway. "Tux is ready to go, studs beside it on the chair."

"Got it," Holly said, turning around, tugging on Harry's tie, beginning to unbutton the model's shirt. She then dropped to her knees in front of him, began untying his shoes. "Come on, come on. No time for modesty, Harry. Kick off the shoes. Drop those pants. We've got to get you into this tux now."

"You want me in a tux?"

Holly looked up at him, motioned for him to slip out of his suit jacket. Nice suit, probably Armani. Modeling must pay even better than she thought. Of course, with this guy's face and body, he could probably command top dollar. "No, I want you in *this* tux, right here, right now. So strip!"

His smile invaded her solar plexus, gave it a punch that nearly sent her toppling over, onto the floor.

"Okay, since you asked. But isn't there somewhere I can change?"

"Yes, there is. Right here. I told you, no time for modesty. Come on, I need you out of those pants."

Harry looked around, saw that nobody really seemed to find anything odd going on and unzipped his suit pants. "Yeah, well, there's a first time for everything, I guess."

Holly paid him no attention, or at least as little attention as possible, because she had noticed that he had great legs. Straight, with unbumpy knees—she hated bumpy knees, because she had them—and with fine dark hair covering his tanned skin. The guy worked out, the guy probably laid in a tanning bed three days a week. The guy wore maroon cotton briefs…

She got up from her knees after holding out the tuxedo pants and watching as he stepped into them, and began fanning herself with one end of the feather boa. She really had to get a grip here.

"Eighth model on the runway. Four minutes, Holly!"

Harry was stuffing his pleated tuxedo shirt into the waistband of his pants as Holly worked to secure the black opal studs. He was still fastening his cuff links as Holly, now standing on a small stool, slid the tie under his lapels, then began tying it. "Hold still, damn it. This is hard enough as it is."

Harry's hands came up, clasped Holly's. "Let me do that, okay," he said, looking straight into her eyes. "I've done it before."

"Yeah, I'll bet you have. Fill in the employment gaps as a professional escort, do you, Harry? You know, taking rich old ladies to the opera, stuff like that?"

"I have taken a few mature ladies to the opera, yes," he answered, lifting his perfect chin as he neatly tied the bow tie. "Now, if you'll help me into my jacket— nice tux, by the way—I'll be ready for you to tell me what comes next."

"What comes next," Holly said, then hesitated, cleared her throat, because Harry Hampshire in a tuxedo was enough to make her choke on her own spit. "…what comes next is you take Jackie's arm here, lead her out onto the runway and smile for the cameras."

For a moment, just for a moment, Harry looked nonplussed. Scared, even. "You want me to do what?"

Holly rolled her eyes. "Oh, come on. What did you think it meant when you signed up for this showing? That you'd just get to hide back here, scarf down some free eats? CNN is waiting, and you and Jackie are going to be all over that station on promos this time next week. Now, let Jackie take your arm—her gown's sort of heavy so you have to help her navigate—and just walk on out there, looking at Jackie as if she's a rare, juicy steak and you've been on a chicken diet all month, okay?"

Harry scratched his head, smiled. "You want me to walk out there with this lady, parade around in my tux, make a jackass out of myself for the cameras?"

"One minute!" Irene said, coming down the few steps from the backstage area of the runway, to stand beside Holly. "Is he ready? Oh my, yes. He certainly is. And I found shoes for Jackie."

"Good," Holly said, then watched as Jackie, keeping her head very straight so that the headpiece and cathedral-length veil didn't topple her backward, laid her hand on Harry's forearm. "Drooling is *not* allowed, Jackie," she bit out, then ran her gaze over both of them, giving them one last check before sending them off. "Irene, weren't there supposed to be bra inserts in this gown? She looks flat-chested."

"I'll get them," Irene said as Jackie glared at Holly.

"Sorry," Holly said, shrugging, knowing she was pointing out Jackie's lack right in front of Harry. "Them that has often notice them that don't. Guess

Mother Nature put those few extra inches in your feet, right, Jackie?''

"Show time," Irene said, fluffing out Jackie's train and veil just as the model looked ready to pick Holly up by her ears, swing her around and launch her toward the snack table. "Let's knock 'em dead!''

Holly stepped back to let Jackie and Harry pass by her up the few steps, then followed, ready to peek out through the break in the curtains once they'd closed behind the two models.

What a sight! The runway, lit romantically by overhead lights, and brightened by what seemed like thousands of photographer's flashes, was filled with Julia Sutherland's designs for what tomorrow's brides should wear.

So many gorgeous gowns, fantastic fabrics. Julia hadn't missed a trick. There were sheaths for the second-time bride, lacy confections for the young bride. There were white, ivory, peach, pink and even one lightest blue gown edged in white lace. Pearls glowed, sequins sparkled. Headpieces of every size and description were matched specifically to each gown. The heady scent of fresh flowers was everywhere as the grooms, each in their own designer tuxedo, made the perfect foils for the perfect brides.

And then, after the first mad explosion of camera shutters was over, Jackie began her walk down the runway, clad in the strapless, backless show gown that seemed to defy gravity, physics and the dress codes for correct bridal wear in at least two out of every three religious denominations.

The material was *peau de soie*, the lace Alencon, and

the style definitely twenty-first century. The skirt of the low-waisted gown had been gathered, as Holly termed it, "six ways from Sunday," pouffing out here, tucked in there, each tuck accented by a small bouquet of pink cabbage roses dotted with faux diamonds. The train went on for miles, the veil for a half-mile more.

This was not a gown to be worn by anyone other than a rock star marrying her tongue-pierced rock star lover, or the movie star tripping down the aisle with her sugar daddy beau. This was grand theater, and Jackie knew it. The press knew it.

And Harry knew he was being upstaged. Definitely. He and Jackie had come to the end of the runway, to stand, be photographed some more, when Harry broke from his "handy place to hang the bride" role and began to ad-lib.

He stepped away from Jackie, but maintained contact by holding onto one of her gloved hands. He gestured toward her, inviting applause from the audience—and it was substantial—then bowed over the model's hand, raising it to his lips.

The crowd applauded again, giving its approval even as Holly, her head barely stuck through the break in the curtains, rolled her eyes and said, "Ham."

But Harry wasn't done. He smiled, winked at the audience, and then pulled the now startled Jackie close, bent her back over one arm and planted one on her.

"I'll kill him," Holly gritted out from between clenched teeth, letting the curtains fall back into place and stomping down the steps to take a quick drink of soda before she had to go out there, take Julia's place and hopefully some bows.

"You're on," Irene said, motioning for her to get back up the steps. She grabbed the pincushion from Holly's wrist, then snagged one end of the boa as Holly tugged in the other direction, spun in a small circle so that the boa unwrapped from her neck, and headed out through the curtains.

She couldn't see a thing. Lightbulbs flashed everywhere, and tall models in huge gowns grabbed at her, hugged her, pushed her forward along the runway, until she got to the end.

Where she stood, dwarfed by Jackie on one side, Harry on the other. She had her speech all prepared, a little something about being honored to stand in for Julia today and thanking everyone for coming.

But the words escaped her as Harry grabbed her, flipped her back over his arm as he had done with Jackie and kissed her square on the mouth.

More lightbulbs flashing, more applause, a little laughter, a few catcalls...and the most overwhelming desire to kiss Harry Hampshire back, and wait a while before killing him.

He released her at last, set her back on her feet, and with the sweep of one hand indicated that everyone should applaud her. "Take a bow, or curtsy if you can manage it," Harry instructed her, speaking around his smile. "Come on, little lady, you've earned it."

"I'm going to kill you," Holly yelled back at him over the applause, a major feat, as she did it while still smiling and without it looking as if she were speaking at all. "Are you nuts? What the hell did you think you were doing?"

"What? You mean you didn't like that? I thought I

was being very inventive. Bridal showing, kiss the bride. All that good stuff."

"Yeah?" Holly said as they turned, Harry having tucked her arm in his as Jackie walked on Holly's other side. "Well, I'm not the bride."

"Well, I am," Jackie pointed out as they neared the curtains once more. "Those of us that can often notice that about those who probably never will," she then said, grinning triumphantly at getting some of her own back after Holly's crack about her lack of cleavage.

"Why, you—" Holly began, then stopped, smiled, as a trio of photographers hopped up onto the runway, eager to take still more pictures. Holly hadn't seen them coming, and now she was blinking furiously, trying to see something other than bright white lights ringed in blue dancing in front of her eyes. "Damn lights!"

"Don't worry, just stick with me. I've got you," Harry told her, guiding her through the curtains, down the steps to the dressing area. He sat her in a chair, then retrieved a can of soda and a cellophane pack of dry crackers from the snacks table. "Here you go. It isn't much, but everything's been pretty well picked over. Do you have to go back out there, face the reporters?"

Holly pressed the cool side of the soda can to her cheek, took a deep breath. "Yes, I do. I do have to go back out there. God, how does Julia manage it? I'm exhausted."

She looked up at Harry, now able to see him again, and wondered if she'd only imagined that kiss he'd given her. Closed-mouth, granted, but it had sure packed a wallop. "I'll be sure to give your name to the CNN people and everyone else. I suppose you've earned a mention in any segments or articles. That was your plan, wasn't it?''

He frowned a little, making this really wonderful crease between his eyebrows—almost as if he might harbor a whiff of intelligence behind that gorgeous face. ''You're going to give them my name? What name?''

''Why, Harry Hampshire, of course. You have others you use professionally? Although I shouldn't help you out, because you nearly gave me heart failure, showing up so late. That really isn't professional, Harry. I could have complained to your agency, and you'd have a hard time getting another job.''

He looked at her for long moments, then sort of shook his head, as if trying to talk himself out of something. Then he said, ''Let me make it up to you. You go do whatever it is you have to do with that thundering horde out there, and I'll get out of this tuxedo. Then I'll take you to dinner. My treat. After all, I made good money here today, right?''

Holly felt a flush running into her cheeks, and hated him for it. Go out with a male model? What did he take her for, a masochist? What woman wants to be seen with a man prettier than her? ''No, I don't think so. I don't date—''

''I'll bet,'' Jackie said, clomping by in a huge aqua turtleneck sweater, tight black leggings and a pair of hiking boots, obviously on her way out as fast as she could go. She had a leather bag the size of Vermont slung over her shoulder, and still wore her full makeup. She looked like Glamour On A Hike.

''Give me fifteen minutes. Twenty, tops,'' Holly said,

Jackie's taunt pushing her into accepting Harry's invitation. "But I want fast food. Hamburger. Fries. A hot dog from a street cart. I don't care. I just don't think I could look at another hotel menu without screaming."

Chapter Two

Colin Rafferty leaned into the mirror as he adjusted the Windsor knot on his maroon-and-navy striped tie.

Funny, he didn't think he looked like a Harry Hampshire.

A Harry Hampshire would wear a silk ascot, or maybe carry a pipe, and have an ugly pug dog that brought him his slippers each evening when he returned home from his job in the moldy recesses of the trust department of the family bank.

Not that it mattered. Today he would be Harry Hampshire. Good old Harry ought to get out more anyway, live a little, see the sights...have some fun with Little Big Mouth, or whatever Julia's employee's name happened to be.

"Hey, excuse me, please," he said, stepping away from the mirror as he saw a semifamiliar face go by. "What's your boss's name?"

"Julia Sutherland," the woman answered. "What else would it be?"

Colin shook his head. "No, I meant the little one— the one with the motormouth."

"Holly?" Irene Collier dropped her chin slightly, "Oops, she wouldn't like it much if she found out I could identify her from that particular description. Still, you're looking for Holly? Holly Hollis. She's number two man—woman—in Sutherland's. She holds us all together."

"Really?" Colin answered, one expressive eyebrow raised. "Well, I don't know about that, Ms.—?"

"Irene, you may call me Irene."

"Irene," Colin repeated, smiling his best "I know I'm bad but you love me anyway" smile. "As I was saying, I don't know about that, Irene. I may not have been here long, but I'm willing to bet today's pay that this whole thing would come tumbling down around everyone's ears if it weren't for your calm head and steady hand."

Now Irene's face turned red, straight up to the thick salt-and-pepper bangs on her forehead. "Well, aren't you perceptive. Okay, what do you want?"

"Nothing much, Irene. Just a little information on our Ms. Hollis?"

Irene hugged the ever-present clipboard to her breasts. "Look, I know she was angry, but it's over now, and forgotten. She isn't going to report you to your agency. In fact, I'll bet she suggests to Ms. Sutherland that we use you again. You were a real hit out there."

"No, that wasn't what I was going to ask you about,

Irene," Colin told her. "Ms. Hollis has agreed to join me for a meal, and I thought perhaps I should know a little more about her. That's all."

Her eyes opening wider, Irene said, "You two have a *date?* No, you don't. Holly would never—never mind."

"Ms. Hollis doesn't date the models?"

"Ms. Hollis," Irene said, rolling her eyes, "thinks male models are a curse and an abomination. Actually she just says they're too pretty and bigheaded for their own good."

"So, what you're saying, Irene, is that if I want to score points with Ms. Hollis, I should go find a bag to put over my head?"

"Oh, you're charming," Irene said, the blush still burning in her cheeks. "She's going to hate you. But, hey, before you go, I want to check through my head shots to find yours, go over the information on the back with you to make sure it's current. We will use you again, I'm sure of it."

Colin slipped into his suit jacket, ran a hand over his collar to be sure it was in place. "Oh, there's no need to do that. It's current. Just send the check to the agency listed on the back. Ah, here comes Ms. Hollis now. Thanks for the information, Irene."

"Sure, anytime. Good luck..." Irene said, already searching through a thick folder of eight-by-ten glossies, looking for Harry Hampshire's photograph.

Colin caught up with Holly as she was thanking the dressers and other backstage help. "Purse, coat and out of here," he whispered into her ear as he took hold of her elbow.

"Hey! What's the rush?" Holly asked him even as he began steering her toward the door. "I've got to talk to Irene, make arrangements for meetings tomorrow. Go find a corner and sit in it, okay?"

"I can't," Colin told her, doing his best to look physically ill. "I'm hypoglycemic. I need meat, protein." He held out one hand, spread his fingers. "Look. See that? I'm starting to get the shakes."

"Oh, for crying out—okay, okay. Maybe it's nice to know you're not quite Mr. Perfect. My coat's the navy one over there on the rack. The one that's shorter than all the others. My purse is looped over the hanger. Just let me talk to Irene for a—hey!"

Colin dragged her along to the coatrack, grabbed the navy wool coat, snagged the large tan purse and aimed Holly at the door precisely five seconds before Irene, paging through her packet of photographs, lifted her head and called out, "Hey! Where'd he go? Hey, did anyone see where that good-looking model went?"

Irene's question was answered by the laughter of two dozen good-looking models....

"So, may I call you Holly? Irene said your name's Holly."

"Sure," Holly said, her head still bent into a strong autumn breeze on the windy streets of Manhattan.

"Okay, and you can call me Harry."

"Well, duh," Holly sniped, shooting him a quick look. "I wasn't going to call you Mr. Hampshire, if you're going to call me Holly. God, that's a lot of *H*'s, isn't it?"

"I think we've pretty much cornered the market,

yes," Colin said, then sort of sighed as Holly bent her head once more, kept walking at a fast clip that had more to do with getting her where she was going than taking a leisurely stroll and getting to know each other better as they walked along. "Are you in some sort of hurry, Holly?" he asked as she couldn't seem to stand still at the corner, waiting for the light to change so they could head across the avenue. She kept looking up at the light, sort of dancing in place.

"You're hypoglycemic," she reminded him. "You've got to eat. Last thing I want is for you to keel over here on the pavement. I'd get trampled by all the women wanting to give you mouth-to-mouth."

"Oh, right," Colin said, smiling slightly, trying to look sick. This was pretty hard to do, considering that the last time he could remember being ill was in the fourth grade, when he'd broken out in spots and couldn't play the second king in the school's Christmas pageant. He'd always thought he'd missed a great opportunity to launch a stage career.

"So, are you feeling any better?" Holly asked as the light turned and they headed across the intersection along with half the population of Manhattan.

"A little better. I...I, um, must have just needed some air."

"But you're still hungry?"

"Still hungry," he answered with a smile as Holly turned into a small restaurant tucked between two upscale shops.

He looked around the restaurant, saw that customers put their orders in and collected them at the same service bar, then carried them to one of the small tables lining one side of the long, narrow room. "Hamburger? Mustard and ketchup? You go find a table, and I'll bring everything to you."

"No, *you* go find a table and sit down before you fall down. I'll order for both of us." She held out her hand, palm up. "You're paying."

"I admire a woman who can still accept money from a man, even while she's ordering him around." Colin fished in his front pocket, pulled out a twenty. "Hamburger, fries, ice water and *no* onions. Just ketchup and mustard. I'm hoping to get lucky later, maybe steal a kiss from a lovely lady."

Holly took the twenty carefully, using only the tips of her fingers to touch a corner of the bill. "Yeah, well, good for you. Me, I'm having onions."

Colin opened his mouth to say something, he wasn't sure what, but Holly was already gone, running to get to the counter before a group of six men who had just come in behind them. That left Colin to locate and commandeer the last free table in the restaurant.

He sat down, used a paper napkin to wipe crumbs from the cracked and scarred wooden surface of the table, then propped his elbows on the wood, rested his chin in one hand.

What in hell was he doing here? Hell, what the hell was he *doing,* period?

Colin hadn't been back to the States for more than a quick visit in nearly three years, enjoying his job setting up one of his second cousin Max Rafferty's overseas holdings, sticking with it until it was up and running properly. Since that holding was in Paris, being overseas hadn't been much of a sacrifice, although he did miss

Max's second wedding to Julia, and had only met her later, when she and Max had flown to Paris for a belated honeymoon.

He'd liked Julia immediately, as anyone who could keep Maximillian Rafferty in line had to be one very terrific lady, and his first stop after going through customs at JFK had been to drop in at the Rafferty condo on Park Avenue. Max had already left the building, and the housekeeper had told Colin that Julia wasn't home, either, so he'd gone off to his hotel, unpacked...and saw the notice for the Sutherland showing in the main ballroom of that same hotel.

A few smiles, a few General U.S. Grant's greasing the right palms, and Colin had been directed to the staging area, where he'd hoped to surprise Julia.

Okay, so that's how he'd gotten there. Now he had to figure out how he'd gotten from there to here, here being sitting in a dingy dive, waiting for his first uniquely American hamburger in too many months.

He was also sitting here waiting for Ms. Holly Hollis, just about the least likely woman he'd ever thought he'd be attracted to, even notice.

But there was something about her. Maybe he'd always harbored a secret fantasy for being bossed around by a pint-size female dictator. Maybe it was the way she'd looked as she stood on a stool to tie his tie, that crazy pink boa wrapped around her neck as she blew at the feathers to keep them out of her mouth, her eyes crossing slightly as she tried to get the knot set correctly.

Or maybe he just wanted to get a little of his own back because she'd mistaken him for some no-show boob named Harry Hampshire. A male model? Did she really think he was a male model?

Good old Harry was in for a surprise, when he got his paycheck for a day's work he didn't do. That was rather amusing. What wasn't amusing was that someone might see him on that television show next week, going by the name of Harry Hampshire, parading around a runway in a tux, kissing women.

He'd have to tell everyone he'd lost a bet. Or won it.

Colin half stood up as Holly approached, balancing a full tray holding several paper-wrapped hamburgers, two bags of French fries and a pair of plastic bottles of spring water.

"Here, let me help you," he said, taking the tray, placing it on the tabletop. Then he held out his hand. "My change?"

"Change? I had to kick in five bucks. What do you mean, *change*. We're in Manhattan, Harry. The lousy water cost three bucks a bottle."

"Sorry," Colin said, fishing into his pocket for another bill. "I guess I lost my head."

"Along with your watch," Holly said as she unwrapped a hamburger, lifted the top of the bun to check for onions, then passed the thing over to him. "I'm waiting, you know. What excuse are you going to give me for almost not making the showing?"

Colin shrugged. Keeping as close as possible to the truth would probably be best. "I'm sorry about that, Holly. I just got in from Paris this morning. There was a slight holdup in Customs."

Holly sat back in her chair and glared at him. "You

just got back from *Paris?* And your agent accepted a booking for the same day? What is he, nuts?''

Colin considered launching into a long story about having been bumped from one plane only to have the second develop engine trouble before they took off, but decided he'd like to get the whole subject gone as quickly as possible, before he slipped up. ''Yeah, that's my agent. Nuts. So, do you live here in Manhattan?''

Holly held up her index finger as she finished chewing, swallowing, her first huge bite of her hamburger. ''Um…no, I don't. I'd go nuts myself, if I had to live in Manhattan.''

''You don't like big cities?''

''Oh, I love them. I love Manhattan. I'd just go nuts here. Visiting museums, taking in all the Broadway and off-Broadway and off-off Broadway shows. Shopping, lots of shopping. Vintage clothing, old books, and we won't even talk about the diamond district. I'd end up being as late for work as you were today, and get myself fired in a month. I mean, a person could make a career out of seeing big cities. Like Paris. I'll bet you did as much sight-seeing as you could?''

''I managed to see a little of the city,'' Colin answered, reaching for a French fry. ''But I sure missed these. How come Americans make better French fries?''

''We use older cooking oil, and more of it,'' Holly supplied, smiling. ''Seriously, you missed American food?''

''Seriously, I did. So, where do you live if it's not in Manhattan?''

''Pennsylvania,'' Holly said, unscrewing the cap on her bottled water. ''Allentown, to be precise. Did you know that the lead actress in *42nd Street* was supposedly from Allentown? The city's used in a lot of songs, books, TV shows. I don't have the faintest idea why. It's just a town. My town, but just a town. Still, with all the new highways, I can be in Manhattan in two hours, so it's still convenient for Julia to check on the plant, or for me to come up here to visit her."

"Julia? That would be Julia Sutherland?"

"Mm-hmm," Holly said, nodding, as her mouth was full once more. For a little person, she sure could eat, and didn't seem to mind letting him know she had a healthy appetite. He bet that Jackie, the model, hadn't eaten an entire hamburger in years, and Holly was already unwrapping her second.

Colin picked up a paper napkin, reached across the table to wipe some ketchup off Holly's chin. "Irene says you're Julia's second in command."

"Irene says a lot, doesn't she?" Holly said, clearly bristling. "What is this? A couple of hamburgers in exchange for whispering in Julia's ear that you want to be headlined in her next showing? Maybe do some print ads in her catalog, even on her Web site?"

Colin sat back, scratched the side of his nose. "What kind of question is that? Do you have that low an opinion of me, or of yourself? Why couldn't I have asked you to dinner because I thought we might enjoy each other's company?"

"Yeah, right," Holly said, poking through the French fries on the hunt for a dark one. "So what's next? You want to take a walk in the park, hold hands, maybe catch a movie?"

"Okay," Colin heard himself say as he crumpled the

hamburger wrappings into a ball and stood up, picked up the tray. "The park first, while it's still got people other than muggers walking the paths."

Holly tipped back her head, looking up at him. He smiled down at her, liking the way she looked at him as if he'd suddenly grown another head. "You really want to make this a real date? Why? I've been rude, obnoxious…"

"Don't forget bossy. Although I have to admit it, I really liked it when you told me to take off my pants."

Holly stood up, shrugged into her coat, then grabbed one last French fry from the tray. "I didn't say that."

"Yes, you did," Colin corrected her. "And you were on your knees when you said it."

"Well, I didn't *mean* it," Holly told him quickly, following him back out onto the pavement. "I mean, I didn't mean it *that* way."

Colin stopped, turned around, put his hands on her shoulders. "I know," he said, then leaned down, kissed the tip of her nose. "Besides, it was the pink boa that got to me. You looked like you were playing dress-up, a little kid in a land of giant dolls."

"I can't help being short," Holly told him as he took her hand, led her across the street and into Central Park. "All us Hollises are short. Mom, Dad, my sister, Helen, my brothers Herb and Harry."

"You've got a brother named Harry? That's a coincidence, isn't it?"

"No, it's just another *H*. We're all *H*'s. Hillary, Howard, Herb, Harry, Helen and Holly Hollis. Looked great on Christmas cards, but that's about it. I swear Helen married John Barker just to get rid of the *H*. I mean, why else would anyone marry a guy who bowls every Thursday night, wearing a shirt that says *Bow-wow Barker* on the back?''

Colin stopped at the entrance to the Park, threw back his head and laughed. "I can't believe it. Your family almost makes mine sound normal."

"And it's not?" Holly asked, pulling him over to a street vendor selling ice-cream sandwiches. "Dessert, and this time it's my treat," she said, reaching into her purse and pulling out her wallet.

"My family? Well, no, it's not. Not in the usual sense, anyway. Mom's an archeologist, and Dad's a professional fisherman. No kidding, there are professional fishermen. I'm their only child, probably because they haven't really lived together very much for thirty years, although they're still married. Dad's in Alaska somewhere right now, fishing, and Mom's in Egypt, digging somewhere near the pyramids."

"Who raised you?" Holly asked, handing him a rather limp ice-cream sandwich.

"My great-aunt and uncle," Colin said, then quickly changed the subject again, because Max's parents had taken care of him when he wasn't in some boarding school. He didn't know how much Holly knew about Max's home life, and didn't want to take a chance on giving her clues she might follow.

"I would have hated that," Holly said as they walked into the park. "We're just this big, noisy family that still gets together every Sunday for dinner. Kids running all over the place, Dad falling asleep in his favorite chair, Mom asking me when I'm going to get married."

"Haven't found anyone worth losing your *H* for,

huh?'' Colin asked, licking at the side of his hand as vanilla ice cream threatened to run into his cuff.

"I'm not really looking," Holly told him shortly. "I've got my career, my own apartment, I'm not thirty yet. I'm in no hurry."

"Well, I'm two years past thirty, but I'm in no hurry, either." He touched her hand again as they walked along, then took it in his, liking the way her flesh felt pressed against his. "Now that we've established that neither of us is chasing a wedding ring, what else do we have in common?"

Holly shrugged, avoiding his eyes. "We both like greasy French fries?"

"Right. Obviously the basis for a firm friendship. And we both like walking in the park as the sun goes down. That's three, not including the hamburgers, or the ice-cream sandwiches. Now, if we share a taste for police chase type thriller movies, we may regret that you got onions on that hamburger. Or that I didn't. There is that, isn't there?"

Holly stopped, looked up at him. "What are you doing?" she asked with the honesty he'd come to recognize, and fear just a little, considering he was being about as dishonest as he could be without wearing a fake mustache and dark glasses.

"What am I doing? I don't know, Holly. I just like you. You're cute, you're prickly, you don't seem to care whether you impress me or not. I like it."

"Oh, I get it now. Women fall all over you, don't they? You have to beat them away with a stick. The male model Adonis. That face, that body—that ego!"

"It all can be a burden, yes. Especially the ego,"

Colin said, sighing theatrically, trying to hide a smile. "Don't hate me because I'm beautiful."

"Oh, *Gawd!*" Holly exclaimed in disgust, letting go of his hand, turning and walking back toward the entrance to the park, Colin hot on her heels.

"Hey, Holly—wait! I was just kidding around," he said, catching up to her. "And don't tell me you didn't want to accept my dinner invitation because I'm a male model, because I won't buy it."

"That is *not* why I tried to turn you down," Holly protested, standing at the corner, tapping her foot as she waited for the light to change.

"Oh? Really? Then tell me, how many male models have you dated? You'd have to have dated some, right, being around them all the time?"

"I have *never*—oh, okay, maybe I have. One." She rolled her eyes. "Three. But that was plenty! Talking about themselves all night long, then having to go home early to get their beauty sleep. Using me to get closer to Julia, to be considered for showings, print ads, you name it. Can't pass a mirror without stopping, checking their hair. Women all but pushing me out of the way to get close to them."

"Have I done any of that?" Colin asked her as they crossed the street together.

"No," Holly admitted, making a face. "But you were at the table while the girl at the counter pumped me about you, wanted to know if I was your *sister*. Do you know how insulting that is? And that girl back there, in the crosswalk. She was going the other way, then stopped dead in the middle of the street, turned around to follow you. She's *still* following us. You turn heads, Harry, don't you know that?''

Colin turned his own head, looked at the woman walking behind him. Pretty, about five foot six, long legs, silky blond hair. She smiled at him. He smiled back. Then realized what he was doing.

"You smiled at her, didn't you?'' Holly asked as they continued walking along the pavement, in the direction of the Waldorf-Astoria.

"Well, of course I did. She smiled at me. I'm not impolite.''

"No, of course you're not. And you can't help it. You're handsome. Drop-dead gorgeous. I'm walking with you, but I might as well be invisible. Models. Male, female. They're just larger than life, too pretty to be real. And you're better than most of them, Harry, no question. I just figure I can have enough of an inferiority complex on my own. I don't need competition from my date.''

"So you don't date models because you think they make you invisible, because you're not some too skinny, plastic, pretty model?''

Holly stopped, stepped in front of him. "I'm not that shallow,'' she told him angrily.

"No, you're not. I never said you were.''

Holly closed her eyes, shook her head. "I'm sorry. You asked me why I don't date models, and I got carried away, got ridiculous. I don't date models, Harry, because I dated one for six months, only to figure out he was in love with himself, not me. So, handsome as you are, nice as you seem to be, and much as I'm attracted to you, this is our first and only date. There, does that answer your question?''

''Pretty much, yeah,'' Colin said, nodding his head. Then he smiled. ''So, you admit you're attracted to me?''

''Oh Lord,'' Holly said on a sigh. ''I'm going in now, Harry. Good night.''

''Wait,'' he said, following her. For a little woman, with short legs, she sure could cover ground in a hurry. ''If we're only going to have one date, don't you think we could make it last longer than an hour?'' He blocked her progress, put his hands on her shoulders, did his best to look comic and soulful at the same time. ''Then I'll always have my memories.''

''Your memories. You're kidding, right?''

''Absolutely,'' Colin agreed, smiling, returning her smile. ''Come on, it's not quite dark yet. Let's walk some more.''

''Only so you can have memories,'' Holly told him as they stepped back out onto the pavement.

They walked along, first hand in hand, then arm in arm, discussing the merits and plot flaws of all the Bruce Willis *Die Hard* movies.

Colin told her about Paris, and Holly told him about her mother who, according to that good woman, still said novenas that her youngest daughter would find a good man, settle down, have a half-dozen kids, forget ''this career business.''

Colin told her about the time he'd traveled around Europe after college, with only a backpack and his ''hitching finger,'' seeing the sights, touring museums, sleeping in youth hostels, getting pie-eyed during Oktoberfest in Germany.

Holly countered with a tale about Girl Scout Camp, and how she'd taken one look at the wooden outhouse and phoned home, demanding her father immediately come and get her. "I can't imagine traveling through Europe with only a backpack. I like my luxuries, and am not afraid to admit it."

He told her about his parents' den, the one with trophy fish on the walls and ancient bits of broken pottery on the tables.

She told him about her mother's collection of ceramic salt and pepper shakers and her dad's pride in having every copy of *National Geographic* ever printed.

They laughed. They argued politics, but only because Colin deliberately disagreed with her for a while, as he got a kick out of the way she looked when she got indignant. They stopped at a small delicatessen and shared a corned beef on rye sandwich between them while the conversation skipped from current events, to books they'd read, to why all boy bands should be bound, gagged and made to promise never to sing again until they could find one note and stick to it.

As they turned yet another corner, and the Waldorf-Astoria was in front of them yet again, Colin had already been mentally kicking himself for about an hour over his deception.

What had started out as a lark had turned into something more. He liked Holly Hollis. He really liked her. She was nothing like any woman he'd ever dated. Cute. Honest. Funny. Short.

And he'd lied to her, continued lying to her. About

who he was, how he'd come to be at the showing. It wasn't as if he hadn't had time to confess, although explaining why he'd gone along with her assumption that he was Harry Hampshire, male model, was still a bit of a mystery to him.

"Well, here we are again," Holly said as they stood just outside the busy entrance to the hotel.

"Yes, here we are," Colin said, looking up, knowing his suite looked out over the front of the hotel.

"I really should go in now," Holly told him, still holding his hands as she faced him. "And you have to catch a cab, right? At least you'll have no problem doing that."

Colin looked at the doorman who stood with a whistle poised between his lips. "Nope. No problem doing that," he said, wondering how he'd tell the cab driver that he wanted to go once around the block. There had to be a big tip involved with that kind of cab ride.

"I had a very good time," Holly told him, avoiding his eyes.

"So did I. Look, Holly—I have to tell you something."

She looked up at him, frowned. "No, you don't. I have to tell you something. I'm sorry. I'm sorry I gave you such a hard time. It wasn't fair of me to automatically not like you because you're a male model. Because you're so damn gorgeous," she added with a little smile.

"Yes, about that—"

"I mean, it's not your fault you're gorgeous. What are you supposed to do? Put a paper bag over your head?"

He grinned. "Actually I had considered it..."

"Please, don't interrupt while I'm apologizing, okay? Why not be a model? Why not think about getting into movies? You'd give Tom Cruise a run for his money, that's for sure."

"Flattery will get you everywhere," Colin said, stepping closer to her. "But the thing is, what happened today was sort of a mistake."

"Oh," Holly said, lowering her eyes, dropping her chin. "Okay. A mistake. I understand."

He put his index finger under her chin, lifted her head slightly. "No, you don't. I'm not saying our date was a mistake. I'm trying to tell you that the showing was a mistake. I never should have—"

"Upstaged the gowns?" Holly asked rhetorically, nodding her head. "I agree. But it was inspired, really. We're going to get some good airtime on that kiss."

"Which one?" Colin asked, momentarily distracted. "The one for the bride, or the one for the lady of the hour—you? Personally I liked the second one best. I never held someone who felt so small, so light in my arms."

"That's because you'd just gotten done flipping Jackie over your arm. Her gown and veil alone probably weigh more than me. But I'm sorry, I keep interrupting you. What are you trying to tell me? What are you sorry about?"

It wasn't going to work. The moment the truth was out, she was going to hit him, kick him, or just burst into tears and run away. He couldn't let her run away, even if he deserved the hit or the kick. What he had to do now was soften her up, make her more willing to listen to him. Cloud her judgment a little, until he could make her understand.

"I'm sorry I didn't kiss you twice," he heard himself say, and the next thing he knew he'd gathered Holly into his arms, and his mouth was on hers.

He could sense when she went up on her tiptoes in order to be able to slide her arms around his neck, and he bowed his body slightly that he could feel the length of her pressed more closely to his body. She was little, yes, but she was all woman. Soft, and curvy, and with lips that knew how to be kissed, how to kiss in return.

Someone exiting the hotel, dragging a large piece of pull-along luggage, bumped heavily against Colin's leg, and the next thing he knew Holly was standing in front of him, her eyes sparkling, her cheeks flushed. "I have to go in now," she said, then pulled a card from her purse and handed it to him. "Here. I'm breaking my own rule. Call me, please?"

"But wait—" Colin called out as she turned and actually began to *run* into the hotel. "I still haven't told you—oh, damn it!" He could see Holly overtop the dozen or more tourists trying to move themselves and their baggage into the hotel, all of them following a tour guide holding up a flag in order to keep the group together. The elevator door stood open, and she rushed inside. "Holly, I—"

"Can I get you a cab, sir?" the doorman asked, and Colin glared at him.

"No, thanks," he said. "I'll walk." And then he followed the tourists into the hotel.

Chapter Three

Holly sat on the thick Persian carpet the day after the showing, holding young Maximillian Rafferty, II—or Max Deuce, as his father sometimes called him—and looked at her good friend and employer. "Julia, it was fantastic. We've got orders pouring in, the press has been very kind. I think it was the snazzy hors d'oeuvres. We served great stuff this time, even if my own taste runs more to little hot dogs in pieces of pastry. I actually saw the reporter from *Women's Wear Daily* tipping a plate of the shrimp-on-a-stick into her purse."

Julia laughed as she pushed a lock of her sleek burnt cinnamon hair behind one ear. "I wish I could have been there, and the little guy seems to be fine today, but I just couldn't leave him yesterday after we got back from the doctor's office. This mom stuff is all-consuming."

Holly looked around the room, furnished in comfortable overstuffed couches, fine antiques and a half dozen colorful infant toys. The condo was huge, two floors and magnificent. It was also a home, a well-loved, lived-in home. "You're doing a bang-up job, Julia. And Max is still so cockeyed over this little guy that I'm surprised he hasn't had him surgically attached to his hip."

"He talked about it," Julia said with a smile as she sipped hot tea from a china cup. "And it doesn't hurt that Max-Two here was born on his daddy's birthday. I don't know if I get any credit here at all."

"Two Leos against one Scorpion," Holly said, shaking her head. "Julia, you don't stand a chance. Although I guess you're going to try for at least one compatible Pisces or Cancer to even things out."

"Oh, definitely. I'm not a slave to this astrology stuff, but I have to admit it, it works on Max. He can be ready to fly into one of his tempers, or go into a pout, and all I have to do is sling a compliment his way and he starts purring like a kitten. Men. They're so..."

"Impossible," Holly ended, then kissed the top of the baby's head. "Except you, of course. You're wonderful."

The baby giggled, pressed his head back against Holly's breasts, blinked his big blue eyes at her.

"Did you see that? Only five months old, and already showing signs of the true Leo. Compliment them and they'll follow you anywhere. And drool on you," Holly added, swiping at little Max's chin with a corner of the soft cloth Julia had tossed over her shoulder when she took Max, telling her that it was either keep a drool cloth handy or be covered with damp spots on her clothing.

"Impossible, Holly? Who's impossible now? Richard? I thought you'd stopped seeing him months ago. Yes, months ago. I've been so caught up with the baby that I guess I haven't been paying attention. Surely there's another man in your life, one you haven't told me about yet?''

"Nope," Holly said, keeping her head down, avoiding Julia's eyes. "Mom's given up on novenas. Last Pop told me, she was thinking about booking a flight to Rome and going straight to the Pope. Like five grandchildren aren't enough for the woman? Why does she think I have to supply her with more?''

"Your mother is a sweetheart, Holly. She can't help it if she believes every woman should be married, having babies. Besides, I kind of agree with her. I didn't know how empty my life was until Max and the baby. Success, a nice income, they're both nice. But you haven't lived until you've seen your sophisticated husband making a complete fool of himself in the delivery room, crying and laughing and handing out cigars. And looking at you as if you've just given birth to the first baby in the entire world.''

"I'll pass, thanks," Holly said, wrinkling up her small, pert nose. "You mothers are all alike. The glories of childbirth. But I watched my sister Helen during all three of her pregnancies. You guys don't seem to mention the indigestion, the swollen ankles, the stretch marks. I'll be an aunt, and be happy to be an aunt.''

"Five bucks, Holly," Julia said, leaning forward on the couch to look deeply into her friend's eyes. "Five bucks says that when you meet the right man the first thing you do is change your mind about babies. Your baby, an adopted baby—any baby at all. Marriage is wonderful, but having a family? Well, it's everything.''

Holly rolled her eyes. "I've got a family, remember? *Big* family. And if you've never sat at the dinner table on Thanksgiving, Christmas—name the holiday—and had that whole big family asking if you have a new boyfriend in your life, and when you're going to settle down so that you, too, can try to eat turkey with a kid crawling all over you? Well, maybe then you'd change your mind.''

Julia took another sip of tea. "It's still Richard, isn't it?''

Holly rolled her eyes. "No, it's not still Richard. Three male models, three strikes, and I'm out! Richard was the last, and I'm over him. *He'll* never get over him, because he's just so gorgeous he can't help himself, but I'm over him. I must have been nuts, thinking someone that drop-dead handsome could ever love me. Thinking someone that handsome was even *capable* of loving someone other than himself,'' she added, sighing.

"But it was you who broke it off, remember, not him. Is he still sending you flowers, trying to make up?''

Holly grinned, Julia's question putting her in mind of an old song. "Nope, he doesn't send me flowers anymore. Or sing me love songs, come to think of it. And, no, I don't regret breaking it off with him. We weren't going anywhere.''

"Aha! You weren't going anywhere. But, according to you, you don't *want* anything to go anywhere. No marriage, no home, no babies on your lap during

Thanksgiving dinner. Holly, you don't *know* what you want, do you?''

"Sure I do. I want to change the subject," Holly said, standing up, handing the baby to Julia. She hated when her friend confused her with logic. "And don't get any ideas out of this, because I'm speaking in general, not personally. But, now that your first showing has been such a hit, I want you to consider a special line of bridal gowns for Petites. Your same great designs, but sort of scaled down for bodies like mine. What do you think?''

"We do use Petites in our ready-to-wear, don't we? But I hadn't considered a special line of Petites for our bridal designs. You may have an idea here, Holly. Let me put Max down for his nap, and I'll be right back to talk about that," Julia said, heading toward the stairs. "Just hold that thought."

Holly was usually an obedient sort, but she couldn't "hold that thought" while she waited for Julia to reappear. She couldn't hold any thought all that long, because one Harry Hampshire was crowding her brain, leaving little room for anything else.

She was attracted to him because he was gorgeous.

Wrong. She was attracted to him because he was funny, and bright, and had this *smile*...

He'd probably practiced that smile in front of a mirror for hours, days, until he'd gotten it right.

He could make her feel so at ease, free to talk, say whatever was on her mind—from politics to what made a good French fry.

He was a model. Self-absorbed, appearance-conscious, always posing, giving meaningful, soulful looks that hid the fact that there might be a light in the window, but nobody was really home upstairs, in his egotistical brain.

He hadn't done the usual model things—insist on a very public dinner in a posh restaurant, a place where he could see, be seen. He hadn't asked for another job, or even for a recommendation.

He was another Richard. Another physically beautiful clotheshorse.

He wasn't another Richard. Richard wouldn't have been caught dead in that greasy spoon restaurant, or have dared possibly dripping ice cream on his designer suit while they walked through Central Park.

He'd kissed her. So what? This was New York. People kissed each other all the time; it was like shaking hands, and sometimes not as intimate a gesture.

He'd kissed her twice. She could still feel the warmth of his mouth against her lips. She could still taste him, remember how it felt to slip her arms around his neck.

She'd made up her mind. She'd never see him again.

Oh God. She'd never see him again...

"All right, I'm ready," Julia said slipping back onto the couch, tucking her long legs up beside her. "Petite wedding gowns. I don't see why not. Tell me what you didn't like about the gowns in the show yesterday."

"I *loved* the gowns in the show yesterday, but I'd only fit into the largest size of the junior bridesmaid's and flower girl styles," Holly said, grateful to be talking business, so that Harry Hampshire had to step behind a curtain in her mind, wait for the next time she masochistically let him on stage again.

"But they don't work for you," Julia said, nodding.

"Only the one—"

"June," Julia said, nodding. She'd designed a dozen bridal gowns for this first showing, and given them the names of the months. "Tight, off-the-shoulder short sleeves, alencon bodice, no sequins, modified A-line skirt, chapel train."

"Right," Holly agreed. "But even that one was about six miles too long. I put it on, and it damn near fell right off again, even zipped. Irene had to gather the material in the back with both hands, just so I could get even a vague idea of how the gown would look if it fit. And I had to stand on two boxes to see how the skirt draped because it was so long. We're talking yards and yards of material being cut away, wasted. The entire bodice would have to be taken apart, put back together, in order to fit me correctly. We're trying for affordable elegance, right? The alterations on that gown, in its smallest size, would cost about half as much as the gown. That's not fair."

"No, it's not," Julia said, pouring both of them second cups of tea. "Stores usually stock several sizes of each gown for brides to try on, order from, but I can imagine how difficult it would be for a size two Petite to try to judge anything while dressed in a size nine Regular. What also isn't fair is the limited selection. A Petite would drown in the more elaborate sleeves, and the amount of tulle in *July's* skirt would make a Petite look as if she'd been attacked by giant ballet tutus. But, Holly, the same goes for larger sizes. The last thing a size twenty-two needs are padded shoulders to hold up pouffy sleeves, or gathers falling straight from the waistline."

Holly watched as Julia picked up her sketch pad.

There were sketch pads all over the condo, in every room, so that when Julia's ideas hit, she had pencil and paper handy to capture her inspiration.

Julia paged through the sketch pad, tossing over pages covered with drawings of blouses, slacks, a really fantastic-looking mother-of-the-bride design Holly had already seen and gushed over earlier. "Okay, here we go. Petites first. Take *April*. Keep the ivory organza, lose the puffed sleeves, give it the same off the shoulder, tight short sleeves as *June*. Get rid of the lace, and replace it—like this."

Holly watched as Julia's pencil flew over the page. "What are those?" she asked, pointing to the horizontal lines her friend had drawn across the bodice and sleeves, all the way down to the dropped waist.

"Folds. Tight, two-inch-wide folds of organza. Pleats, starting at the dropped waist, the folds of each organza pleat rising above the previous fold, all the way to the top of the bodice, and incorporated into the sleeves. Invisible stitching, so that the look is smooth. Instead of lace, or diamanté, or beads, we use the fabric for bodice interest. Elegant, but simple. Completely, utterly without decoration. We keep the skirt plain, keep the fullness, with two deep pleats edging the hem. Cathedral train, because now even a smaller bride can carry that off, with the rest of the gown so simple."

"And a simple cathedral veil, edged in one of those pleats? No real headpiece, just the veil sewn to an invisible comb," Holly suggested, and Julia drew it, captured the veil in a few swift strokes. "Perfect! I'd wear that."

"If you got married, which you say you're never going to do," Julia pointed out, closing the sketch pad.

Holly winced. She'd gotten Julia off the subject, then stupidly brought her right back to it. They'd joked, earlier, about Julia's two Leos, which should have reminded Holly that Julia was a textbook case Scorpion, who'd never seen a secret she couldn't ferret out if she just tried long enough.

"Ah, I saw that wince. Yes, Holly, we're back to our original subject now," Julia said, smiling. "Did you really think I'd let go so easily? Because you met somebody, didn't you, Holly? Come on, confess. One of the models hit on you yesterday, right?"

"Okay, okay, so I met somebody," Holly admitted, sighing. She might as well 'fess up and get it over with, because Julia was going to keep coming at her until she told her every last detail. "And, yes, it was at the showing yesterday. Harry Hampshire. His name is Harry Hampshire."

"E-gods, I hope that's his professional name," Julia said, grimacing. "What this world does *not* need is a Holly Hollis Hampshire. Of course, all those *H*'s never hurt Vice President Hubert Horatio Humphrey, right?"

"Would you cut that out?" Holly said, flopping back against the soft cushions of the couch. "It's bad enough I went out with him."

"To die for, huh?" Julia asked, raising her eyebrows.

"Our own videotape of the show will be delivered here this afternoon, so you can judge for yourself. But, yes, definitely to die for. If I were that shallow."

"Sweetie, we're *all* that shallow. Gorgeous is gorgeous. Is he nice?"

Holly felt her cheeks growing hot. "Yeah, he is. Nice." Then she shook her head. "But he's not for me. I'm not going down that road again. It's a dead end."

"Did he ask to see you again? Did he kiss you good-night?"

"What? You're writing a book now, Julia?" Holly asked, getting up from the couch, beginning to pace. "We had hamburgers and fries, took a walk through the park, talked and he kissed me good-night. End of story."

Julia shifted slightly on the couch, putting a hand on her ankle and pulling her legs up closer beside her. "He kissed you good-night. Ah. And did you kiss him back? Open mouth or closed? Details, Holly. I'm an old married woman now, and I need to take my thrills were I can find them."

"Oh, yeah, right. You're married to Max Rafferty, one of the most sinfully handsome men of this or any millennium, and *you* need thrills? Give me a break."

"Open mouth," Julia decided, grinning. "Definitely open mouth."

"You're impossible!"

"And you're blushing. Oh, Momma Hollis will be so happy. Now, come on, I don't want to wait for the videotape. Besides, you're so good at description. Describe him for me, Holly. Do it with movie stars."

Holly gave in and gave up. She wanted to talk about Harry. She was dying to talk about Harry. "Movie stars? Okay. But only to keep you happy. Hair and eyes? Tom Cruise. Definitely Tom Cruise. Straight hair, the kind that falls forward on the guy's forehead, so that your hands just *itch* to sweep it back for him. Those same sort of flyaway eyebrows low over—God, the *bluest* eyes.''

"Keep going," Julia urged. "I'm getting a mental picture here."

"What? Cruise's eyes and hair aren't enough for you? Okay, we travel down to the nose. Whose nose? Not Matt Damon's. It's more patrician than that. Slim, straight, but with the sexiest bumped-out thing to it. Sort of hawklike, but classy. I know—Paul Newman. He'll *never* be too old for me!"

Julia narrowed her eyes. "Don't both Paul and Tom pretty much have the same kind of nose?"

"I know, I'm trying for variety here. Mouth... definitely George Clooney's mouth and chin. And he smiles like Clooney, too, so that the skin around his eyes kind of crinkles up and you just know he's thinking something absolutely delicious." Holly waved a hand in front of her face. "Is it getting warm in here?"

Julia collapsed against the couch cushions, giggling.

"All right, the grand finale. He's got this *body*. I mean, does he have this *body*. Tall, slim, but muscular. Broad shoulders, but not out of proportion to the rest of him. He's even got great knees."

"Knees?" Julia sat up again, obviously paying close attention, even through her giggling. "And how, Holly, do you know about his *knees?*"

Holly went down on her own knees, tried to make herself look busy as she gathered up the soft velour throw little Max had been lying on, the few toys scattered on it. "I sort of...I sort of took off his pants."

"You sort of took off his *pants?* No, no," Julia said,

erasing her words as she wiped a hand in the air. "I'm not going to interrupt. Go on. Tell me."

Sighing, Holly remembered that she'd already known she was going to have to tell Julia the whole story. The whole miserable, embarrassing story. She was only surprised Julia hadn't pulled out a tape recorder, to preserve Holly's embarrassment for posterity. "He wore maroon briefs," she ended a few minutes later, as Julia was reaching for a box of tissues, wiping at her streaming eyes. "Have you ever thought of a line of men's underwear, Julia. Because, if you have, have I got the model for you!"

"Oh, Lordy, Lordy," Julia chortled, dabbing the tissue under her eyes, careful not to smudge her mascara. "Only you, Holly. *Take off your pants.* And you actually *said* that to the man?"

"While I was on my knees in front of him, trying to untie his shoes, yes. It wasn't one of my better moments, I grant you, but we only had a couple of minutes to get him into the tuxedo. I doubt he took it personally."

"No, of course not," Julia said, shaking her head. "He only laid one on you right on the runway. He only asked you for a date right after the showing. I doubt he had a single idea in his head at all."

"He kissed me, yes," Holly said quietly. "But on the runway it was for the cameras, and then later, when he'd walked me back to the hotel—which meant nothing. What was he going to do? Shake my hand? It was a date. He kissed me good-night."

"The cad," Julia said, giggling.

"Okay, okay, so I liked it. I liked *him*. But nothing

is going to come of it, because I'm not going to *let* anything come of it. No more models, Julia. I took an oath. Never again will I date anyone prettier than me. I even embroidered it on a pillow somewhere. Or I would have, if I could embroider."

Julia closed her eyes, shook her head. "You gave him your card, didn't you?" she asked, then sighed. "Holly, you're transparent, you poor thing. And I'm just betting you gave him your card."

Holly bent her head, rubbed at her forehead. "You ought to set up shop on Forty-second Street, Julia. See all, know all, tell all. How do you do it?"

"Because you're transparent, remember?" Julia repeated. "And, even though you'll never admit it, you're a born romantic. Has he called yet?"

"No, he hasn't called me yet," Holly said, knowing her cell phone was in her pocket, fully charged, and turned on. "And I'm not so sure I want him to call, to tell you the truth."

"Yes, See All, Know All Julia also sensed that. But, Holly, you can't lump all male models, or all men, into one category, that category being Untrustworthy. Because that's your problem, Holly. You don't trust men. You don't trust yourself to know a good relationship from a bad one. You don't trust your own heart, or your own motives. Stop me anytime here, Holly."

"I can't," Holly said, collapsing onto the couch once more. "I can't, because you're right. I don't trust men. Your Max and my dad are the only two good examples I have of trustworthy men."

"And my dad," Julia added.

"Right, and your dad. But Helen's John? Oh, he

swears it will never happen again, and he's been good for about five years now, but Helen was nearly destroyed when she found out about his gambling. They nearly lost the house, remember?''

"I think you're confusing trustworthiness with human frailty. John had a problem, and he licked it. That's commendable.''

"Sure,'' Holly said, nodding her head. ''But he didn't tell Helen until they were flat broke and the electricity was turned off. He just kept saying he'd been paying the bills, when he'd actually been betting on football. Helen still keeps the checkbook, because as much as she loves him, she can't quite trust him. Then there's Harry.''

"Harry Hampshire.''

"No, Harry Hollis, my big, dumb brother,'' Holly corrected. ''Or have you forgotten that time he took his secretary with him for a business conference in Las Vegas? Monkey business. Janet forgave him, I don't know how, but she still doesn't trust him and it's been three years. Now imagine a guy who looks like Harry—Hampshire this time—set loose in a world of secretaries and whatever. Just the thought makes my skin crawl.''

"I think I see where this is going,'' Julia said, munching on a slice of buttered whole wheat toast that had gone cold at least an hour earlier. ''But your brother Herb never cheated on Nancy. And you never said he gambles. So, tell me, what's his fatal flaw?''

"Herb?'' Holly shrugged her shoulders. ''Okay, so he's one of the good guys, too. There's *lots* of good guys. I know that. And Richard only cheated on me with himself—definitely more in love with himself and his good looks than he could ever be with any woman.''

"Yes, now I definitely see where this is going,'' Julia said quietly. "You are talking about trust, Holly, but that's only a part of it. You want to be the center of some man's universe, don't you? You want him to love and trust you, you want to love and be able to trust him. You want honesty, complete and utter honesty. More so, being a Cancer, you crave security. And, sadly, because you've been burned a couple of times in the past, and because of examples you've seen in your own family, you don't seem to think you'll ever get it. How am I doing?''

"I think I should never have loaned you that book on the Zodiac,'' Holly grumbled, crossing her arms under her breasts. "Maybe it's because I was number four, the youngest child in the family. Maybe I missed out a little on being special, being the center of someone's universe—although, for the past five years or so, I've been wishing my mother would give me a little *less* attention. But you have to remember, Julia, I *am* a Cancer. So I'm moody and self-pitying and full of uncertainty. Oh, and terribly overdramatic, a real live drama queen. All that good stuff.''

"Yes, and you also have infinite patience, you could persuade rain to fall upward, and you're loving and sensitive, as well as fairly brilliant and original. You're so organized you could successfully herd cats, you're open and honest and sometimes brutally frank, and you're the most *loyal* person I've ever met. Oh, and you get along best with Pisces, Scorpio—that's me—and Taurus. I'm afraid that's all I've got, but I can pull out that book for you if you can find out Harry Hampshire's sign.''

"Very funny," Holly said, trying hard not to slip into one of her "pity me" moods, moods she'd learned to control since her rather turbulent teenage years. "But it doesn't matter what his sign is, because I'm *not* going to allow myself to become involved with another male model. You listed my good and bad traits, Julia, but I didn't notice 'deliberately bangs her head against stone walls' anywhere.''

"But you'd still consider a handsome man, if he *wasn't* a male model?" Julia asked, and something in the tone of her voice alerted Holly that, contrary to what she'd thought, she and Julia weren't just having a girl-to-girl talk.

She pulled her legs up onto the couch cushion and turned to her friend. "Okay, spill it. It's Max again, isn't it? Whose cousin's sister-in-law's oldest boy is coming here today for lunch? A nice boy. A lawyer, maybe a doctor. Come on, Julia, tell me. Max is doing it to me again, isn't he? He's matchmaking again, isn't he?''

"No!" Julia exclaimed, then averted her eyes. "Okay, yes, he's doing it again. But you'll like Colin, honestly you will. He's intelligent, *extremely* successful, comes from a good family—Max has a wonderful family, you know. I guess his only drawback, if you can call it a drawback—and I know you will—is that Colin is quite handsome. Quite handsome,'' she ended, actually wincing.

"Colin? I don't remember that name.''

"Sure you do, Holly. It's Max's cousin, Colin Rafferty."

"Oh God, another Rafferty. Save me from another Rafferty. You can handle Max, but you're a Scorpion. An insecure Cancer would be running for the hills...which is what I'm going to do now, because you have invited this Colin guy here for lunch today, right?"

"Maybe," Julia admitted. "Possibly, if Max found him at his hotel. He only got into New York yesterday, and we've been playing phone tag ever since, unfortunately. Please, Holly, stay. Max will be back soon."

"All right, don't beg. It's so unbecoming," Holly teased. "But I still want to be on the road back to Allentown tonight, tomorrow morning at the latest. So don't let Max try to fix us up, okay? I mean, you do remember the fiasco with Max's third cousin's son?"

"Bruce? Oh, yes, I remember. Who knew a guy with three degrees in computer science could have that many hands?"

"And very limber fingers, probably from all that typing," Holly said. "Do you know how difficult it was for me to have to tell Max that I bopped his cousin over the head with his own laptop as we drove back from the theater? Bruce said he couldn't help himself, he was overcome with emotion after watching the show. We saw *Cats,* for crying out loud! That guy was just plain oversexed."

"And very underloved, by you," Julia said with a smile, arranging cups on the silver tray and getting ready to return everything to the kitchen. "He went back to Iowa the very next morning, with Max still roaring in his ear all the way to the airport, poor thing. Max apologized to you.''

''Yes, he did. He apologized, he sent flowers, he sent fruit-of-the-month selections, he sent me a box of New York strip steaks. The man apologized until I begged him to stop. And then he introduced me to his accountant's son, Dennis. Max just doesn't *learn*, Julia.''

''I agree, he doesn't. He's very persistent, which is why I'm so very happily married to him instead of still pretending I don't love him. But I promise, Holly, this is the last time. I'll tell him—no more fix-ups, okay?''

''Like I have a choice?'' Holly grumbled, once more feeling one of her bad moods trying to slip over her. She fought it off. ''So, you said this Colin guy just got into New York yesterday? Where's he from?''

''Texas,'' Julia answered as Holly, carrying little Max's empty bottle, followed her friend into the kitchen. ''Well, originally from Texas. He's lived just about everywhere, I believe, as his parents get around a lot. But, for the past few years, Colin has been handling—brilliantly, I might add—Max's overseas companies. He was headquartered in Paris, if you can believe that. We met him there, on our second honeymoon.''

''Paris?'' Holly said, unscrewing the baby bottle lid and tossing the lid and nipple into a jar of soapy water Julia always kept beside the sink. ''Did you say Paris?''

''Mm-hmm,'' Julia told her, rinsing cups and saucers and placing them in the dishwasher. Julia had a live-in housekeeper, but she'd been raised to ''do'' for herself, and enjoyed taking care of her own house. ''Why? Do you remember now? Because I told you how Colin took us to all these wonderful out-of-the-way restaurants tourists never see.''

''Paris,'' Holly repeated, her stomach twisting in a knot even as her arms and legs started this sort of *tingle*…a sort of early-warning system she'd developed that warned her when she was about to be *very* unhappy. ''And he's gorgeous?''

''Yes, Holly, he's gorgeous. Remember that old advertising line? Don't hate me because I'm beautiful?''

''Remember it? I think I just heard it yesterday,'' Holly said, heading back to the living room, ready to grab her purse and run. There were just too many coincidences here.

''Holly, where are you going? You promised to stay.''

''I know, Julia, but I just remembered that…I forgot that…oh, hell, Julia, please just let me leave.''

''Too late,'' Julia said, lifting her head slightly as the sound of Max's voice came to them from the foyer.

''Julia? I've got Colin with me. I had a devil of a time convincing him that he wasn't barging in and that Max-deuce is fine now. Is Holly here? Because I told Colin that I really want him to meet—hi, Holly, honey,'' Max ended as he entered the living room.

''Hi, Max,'' Holly said, picking up her purse and heading for the door. ''Hi, Harry,'' she said, stopping in front of Colin.

Then, before he could do more than open his mouth to say something to her, she stepped back, took aim and *whapped* him a good one across the chest with her purse before running out of the condo.

Chapter Four

Colin sat on the edge of the couch, his hands covering his ears in a sort of mock self-defense—maybe as a sort of *real* self-defense, because the air around his head had been rather blue for a while.

Max had been going after him for about twenty minutes now—once Julia had gotten through with him—and showed no signs of running down. Colin was a jackass, an idiot, the worst of the worst, cruel and immature, the lowest of the low—and those were his *good* points.

But, finally, even the great Maximillian Rafferty ran out of insults, probably because he was momentarily distracted as Julia brought the young Rafferty heir into the living room and thrust him at his adoring father.

Colin took his hands away from his ears and was just about to heave a sigh of relief when Julia sat down beside him on the couch.

"Okay, so now that Max has finished—you *are* fin-

ished, darling—what are you going to do now, Colin?"
she asked him. She looked so innocent, sounded so rational, that Colin still had trouble believing his cousin
Max had once worn a plate of linguine in clam sauce
over his head, a parting gift from the ladylike Julia
Sutherland Rafferty before she walked out of his life for
nearly five years.

Colin shrugged, hoped to find the right words to keep
Julia looking as cool and unruffled as she sounded.
"Find her? Apologize?"

"Grovel at her feet? Throw yourself in front of the
Park Avenue bus?" Max growled unhelpfully. "No,
better. *I'll* throw you in front of the Park Avenue bus."

"Now are you done, darling?" Julia asked, smiling
up at her husband. "Because I think it's Colin's turn to
speak. Colin?" she asked, directing her cool brown
stare at him, as if she expected him to perform like some
trained dog. "Speak."

Standing up, putting some prudent space between
himself and both his cousin and Julia, Colin tried to dig
out, just a little, from beneath the mess he'd piled up
since arriving in New York City.

"Look, it just *happened*. I came here, Julia, to see
you guys, and the housekeeper told me you were out.
Okay, so I left a message, told you I'd be checking in
at the Waldorf, and me and the limo you sent to the
airport went over there." Colin's grammar, always me-
ticulous, was suffering badly. But, then, he was operating under some duress.

"So I get to the Waldorf, and I see this placard in
the lobby about your showing. I found my way to the
staging area, dressing rooms, whatever you want to call

it, and the next thing I know this *woman* is grabbing me by the arm, telling me I'm late, and ordering me to drop my pants. She damn near pulled them off me.''

Max's attention was at last redirected from tickling his son under the chin. ''She said *what?* She did *what?*''

''Oh, dear. It doesn't sound quite so funny hearing Colin tell it,'' Julia remarked, wincing.

''Exactly! That's the same thing I thought, Max. I thought—*what?*'' Colin said, pointing a finger at Max and ignoring Julia's comment, because he hated to think about how the story had been told from Holly's perspective. ''Now I ask you, Max—what would you have done? I tell her she's made a mistake, and she's going to go ballistic because she's just made a fool of herself with Max Rafferty's cousin. Besides, they were short one model, and she needed help. She really *did* need help. I was there, I was available—the tux fit. So what would you have done, Max? Tell me.''

Max looked at his wife. Colin could almost see his cousin's brain working, smell the smoke as the gears turned. ''Nothing,'' Max said. ''I would have done and said nothing. I would have gone along with it, at least for the moment. You really didn't have much choice, not with your pants hanging around your ankles.''

''Except you would, at the first opportunity after the showing, explain who you are, so that there'd be no misunderstanding,'' Julia supplied helpfully.

Max immediately looked guilty. ''Right. Er, right! That's exactly what I would have done. The moment the showing was over, I would have explained everything. Definitely.''

''Oh, give me a break,'' Julia said, shaking her head.

"You would have done the same thing Colin did. I've already heard this story, from Holly's perspective, and believe me, Colin was actually rather restrained in his response. Poor frazzled, deluded, desperate Holly on her knees, tugging at his suit pants. Colin basking in the thought he'd been mistaken for a top male model. *Maroon* briefs." She rolled her eyes. "I can just picture it."

"Um, Julia?" Colin asked quietly. "I know you're trying to help here, and I thank you. But please don't tell me you can picture me in my underwear. Max is listening, and I kind of like having all my own teeth."

Julia looked at her husband. "Oh. Sorry," she said, then grinned. "Besides, I'm not letting you off the hook just yet, Colin. I can understand that you were having fun, going with the moment and all of that. But you had plenty of time to correct Holly's mistake, and you didn't. That's what I find so inexcusable."

"So do I," Colin agreed, rubbing at his abdomen. Not that it really had hurt when Holly slugged him with her purse, but for a woman who probably couldn't weigh much more than one hundred pounds, she sure did pack a wallop. "I guess you would have had to have been there. I don't remember the last time a woman was so open, so honest with me. Not trying to impress me, not flirting and sending out lures, not—"

"We get the idea," Max bit out shortly.

"And at least one of those *we* is getting nauseous," Julia added, smoothing down her skirt as she stood up. "You poor, poor Rafferty men, so horribly cursed with their beauty. Give me that child, Max," she ordered, holding out her hands toward her baby. "I'm going to take him into the kitchen to feed him. But you two stay here. I don't want him to hear any more of this. He's young, and impressionable.''

Max waited until his wife had disappeared in the direction of the kitchen, then grinned at his cousin. "So you like her, right?"

"Oh God," Colin all but groaned. "Here we go. Yes, Max, I like her. And I was going to find her later today, tell her the truth, explain everything over dinner in some very public place, so she couldn't scream at me or throw things. I had it all worked out in my mind."

"Really? Obviously you don't know Holly that well. She probably would have pelted you with the dinner rolls, then stomped out of the restaurant. Which is a lot less lethal than anything my wife would have done to me in the same circumstances, but Holly's a nice person."

"And Julia isn't?"

"My wife is a wonderful person, Colin," Max said, grabbing them each a bottle of water from the small refrigerator built into the bottom of a cherry buffet table. "But she has a very well-defined notion of quid pro quo. You quid, and she pro quos you—double. Sometimes triple. Did I ever tell you about the linguine with clam sauce?"

"Yes, you did. So Holly wouldn't go that far?"

Max unscrewed the lid of his water bottle, frowning. "No. No, she wouldn't. She'd blow, definitely. But then she'd get very sad. Not that my wife can't be hurt, because she can. But Holly can turn being hurt into a real production number, complete with tears, sulks and more slammed doors than you'd want to know about, trust me. She makes a great show of being angry, but mostly she's hurt. Holly's a lot of bluster, but she's very vulnerable. Not fragile, but vulnerable. You hurt Julia and you get hurt back, in spades. You hurt Holly, Colin, and I expect you're going to have to do some major groveling before you can make things right again. You do want to make things right again, don't you?''

"I do," Colin said, nodding his head. "After all, it's my fault."

"Yes, it is your fault," Max agreed. Damn Max for always being so agreeable when Colin was the one looking bad. "But don't do it just for me, or for Julia. Things are bad enough now. Don't lead Holly on, okay? Just be honest."

Colin tried to explain himself, just one more time. "She was going on and on about models—male models mostly—and how they're so vain and how she feels, well, insecure around them. And the whole time she didn't even notice that heads turned as we walked by, especially while she was eating that damn ice-cream sandwich. One guy nearly walked into a pole, watching her lick vanilla ice cream off her fingers. She's cute, she's funny and she's sexy as all hell. All of it wrapped up in this tiny, yet rather volatile package."

He shook his head. "Now tell me, Max. How was I going to throw a monkey wrench into a wonderful evening by telling her the truth? It was just a whole lot simpler at the time to be Harry Hampshire."

"She's staying at the Waldorf, like you," Max said after a moment.

"I know. I'll head there now," Colin said, feeling

about as ready to move as a rabbit with a fox in the vicinity. "Maybe flowers? Candy?"

"Your head on a platter might work," Julia said, reentering the living room, young Max on her shoulder as she patted the baby's back. "You might want to give her a little more time to blow off steam, Colin, and to have a good cry. Besides, I doubt that she went back to the hotel, because you know she's staying there. If I know Holly, she's at the Frick, sitting in the enclosed courtyard, trying to calm herself. She really loves the Frick."

"The Frick?" Colin asked, frowning.

"The Frick Collection, an art museum," Max told him. "On East Seventieth Street, at the park. You can walk there from here on a nice day like this, which is probably why Julia's so sure Holly went there."

Colin headed for the foyer, then stopped, turned around. "Thanks, guys, and I'm sorry. I'm very, very sorry, and I'll fix it."

"Of course you will, Colin," Julia said encouragingly. "But just one favor before you go, if you don't mind. What sign are you?"

"What sign am I?" Colin, his head full of too much information as it was—and stuffed even fuller with questions—answered blankly, "Sign of the Zodiac? Isn't that question sort of old hat now? I thought it died out with the last millennium."

"Tell her your sign, Colin," Max said calmly, although a smile hovered at the corners of his mouth.

"It's Taurus. Why?"

Julia smiled sweetly. "No reason. Taurus. How nice.

Call us later and let us know how you make out, Colin, all right? Don't forget."

"Sure," Colin promised, then headed toward the door once more. If Holly was at the Frick, he'd go to the Frick. If Holly was on the moon, he'd go to the moon. Hell, he'd go to the moon on his own if he didn't go after Holly, because Max would boot him straight into outer space.

It was a nice day for a walk in Manhattan. The sun was warm, the breeze mild and the lunchtime crowd remarkably polite as they made their way along the sidewalks. Colin stopped at a small grocery store that had an outside display of bouquets, picking one made up of butter-yellow chrysanthemums that caught his eye.

Holly would either accept them, or bash him over the head with them...which is why he decided not to buy her anything as dangerous as a five-pound box of chocolate truffles. A solid brass paperweight of the Statue of Liberty, also on sale at the counter of the grocery store was, of course, entirely out of the question.

As he walked along, in his hand-tailored navy suit, his dark sunglasses shielding his eyes from the sun, the breeze doing a small dance in that one lock of hair that always seemed to fall forward onto his forehead, Colin was blissfully unaware that he had made the days of at least three secretaries, and gladdened the heart of one octogenarian who still had a very good memory of her younger, more flirtatious days.

It was like that for Colin. Sometimes he *knew* when he was causing a stir. It was rather hard not to know. But, mercifully, for the most part he was unaware of stares, covert looks, hands lifted to feminine mouths to cover girlish giggles.

Because he was Colin Rafferty. He knew he had this certain *appeal* to the feminine mind or heart or whatever, but he had learned to never let it go to his head. He couldn't. He was much too busy living his life, enjoying his career.

Okay, so he wasn't beneath using a well-aimed look, a perfectly timed smile, when it got him what he wanted, where he wanted to go. Only a jerk would look a gift horse—or a handsome face—in the mouth.

And he hadn't always been so unaware of the power of his physical looks.

From the time he'd been handed over to his third or fourth nanny—at about the age of five—he'd figured out that women liked him. They catered to him, liked to feed him milk and cookies, liked to help him with his homework.

For a while, during his teenage years, he'd become more than a bit of a jerk. Females flocked to him, and he wasn't yet mature enough to resist the urge to take advantage of them, injure their tender hearts.

Until Max had gotten wind of what was going on, that is, and just about taken Colin apart. And he'd learned. He learned that an almost perfect "outside" meant nothing, less than nothing, if the "inside" didn't live up to its "cover."

So Colin had stopped posing, and started to crack open the books. He still played on his high school baseball and football teams, but he also joined the debate club. He painted scenery for the class play, took guitar lessons with more of an eye to the classical than the quick chording that wowed the girls as he played and sang vocals with a local rock band.

The high school girls still chased him. And then the college girls chased him. And then women, all sorts of women, from Texas to New York, to Paris, and everywhere in between. Except he didn't let so many of them "catch" him anymore. He was careful not to take everything that was offered to him, learned to judge others as he wished to be judged.

In short, Colin grew up.

Just to have a major relapse yesterday, with a woman who, he had to admit to himself, just might be the one woman in the world who would actually *dislike* him because his face didn't scare small children.

No wonder he was intrigued. For all the good it would do him.

He crossed the street and saw the Frick in front of him, a large, imposing building he was amazed he'd never noticed on his earlier trips to Manhattan.

So this was where a Holly Hollis would go when she wanted to be alone? Interesting.

He stepped inside, felt the coolness of being surrounded by very thick walls, aware of entering a sort of haven far removed from the hustle and bustle of the New York City streets. Paying his entrance fee, he was handed a brochure that included a map of the museum as well as a short history.

Stalling, playing for time, he opened the brochure, and learned that a man by the name of Henry Clay Frick, a Pittsburgh, Pennsylvania coke and steel industrialist, had ordered the construction of this huge mansion around 1913, for use as a private home. Some private home. A guy could fly a kite right here in the foyer.

Henry had willed the building and his art collection to a trust, and that trust had added considerably to Henry's already impressive collection, so that now over one thousand, one hundred works of art were on display. A Rembrandt. An El Greco. Some Whistler.

Colin was always impressed to learn that private citizens actually owned great masterpieces, and only loaned them to museums from time to time.

He could imagine—just barely—what it would be like to eat dinner in a dining room overlooked by El Greco's *Storm Over Toledo,* or some such work of art. It would be kind of difficult to munch hot dogs while in the presence of such a masterpiece. Of course, people who had masterpieces in their dining rooms probably didn't eat hot dogs anyway.

"You're stalling when you should be moving, Rafferty," he said out loud, refolding the brochure and stuffing it in the inside pocket of his suit jacket. Transferring the green paper-wrapped bouquet to his left hand, he set out in the direction of the large inside courtyard, which rather dominated the area just inside the entrance.

Magnificent. The courtyard was magnificent, all soaring columns and architectural touches that would have turned heads even in Paris.

He'd have to come back here one day, when his mind was ready to concentrate on more than finding Holly, explaining himself to Holly. Groveling to Holly.

And then he saw her.

She was sitting on a stone bench at the far side of the reflecting pool, her back to him as she looked up at a group of columns with an intensity that made him wonder if she was thinking of climbing one of them.

She looked great. That probably had something to do with the fact that she wore Sutherland designs—today, cocoa-colored, heavy silk slacks and a cream-colored sweater with a soft cowl collar. But mostly she looked great because she seemed so at home in her own skin.

She wore her shiny cap of chestnut hair in a style that said, "If you don't like it, don't look." He liked it, and he looked.

Even as her back remained turned to him, he remembered how open and honest her huge green eyes looked as she'd told him bits and snatches of her life. He remembered that intriguing, slightly pointy chin that she kept lifting, jutting out, daring the world, or him, to say something that needed a rebuttal.

She didn't pose, or primp, or give any indication that she cared what anyone thought of her. And yet he knew, not just because Max had told him so, that Holly Hollis was not half as brash and secure as she'd like the world to believe.

And he'd hurt her. He hadn't needed Max nor Julia to tell him that, either. He'd seen the hurt in those huge green eyes as she'd said, "Hi, Harry," and right before she'd belted him with her purse.

He thought back over their date of the previous evening. What they'd said, what they'd shared. Her honesty, his deception. This wasn't going to be easy, and he doubted one bouquet of yellow posies was going to cut it, even if coupled with his best "you know you love me" smile. *Especially* if he accompanied the flowers with the smile he'd used to such great effect with the ladies before he'd learned it wasn't fair to do that, use the charm and face he'd been born with to unfair advantage.

So he stood there, his feet all but nailed to the floor, scared to death of one small woman he probably outweighed by seventy pounds, towered over physically. Scared to approach her, scared to see her look at him, look through him, look at him in disgust for his dishonesty, his deception.

Scared to see the hurt in her eyes again, knowing he was the cause of that hurt.

And then it hit him. *He* knew she'd been hurt. *She* knew she'd been hurt. But it would probably be fatal to act as if he *knew* she was hurt. He had to think about her as being angry—rightfully angry, mad as hell. Because, if she was hurt, that would mean that her emotions were somehow involved, and Holly probably would rather poke a sharp stick in her eye than admit that Harry Hampshire, the louse, had the power to hurt her.

At least that's what Colin decided, then went with, quickly, before he could go over the thoughts in his head one more time, which probably would just confuse him. Tossing the flowers in a nearby trash can, he strolled to the end of the courtyard and sat down beside Holly. "Hi. Come here often?"

"Go away."

"No, seriously. Do you come here often? Is this one of the places you'd spend all your time in if you lived in the city? What about Modern Art? Do you like Modern Art?"

"If you mean, do I like blackened banana skins

stretched out and mounted on a wall to represent the shrinking world and the vagaries of the economy, no, I don't like Modern Art. There, I've answered your question. *Now* go away."

"Nope," Colin said, leaning back slightly, wrapping both arms around one raised knee. "First I'm pretty sure I need you to yell at me."

She turned her head toward him, then faced the pillars once more. "I don't want to yell at you," she said, her voice low, for they were, after all, in a museum. "I have absolutely no desire to yell at you."

"Sure you do," Colin told her bracingly. "Yell, scream, tell me what a bastard I am, tell me to go to hell. Come on, Holly. I know you're mad."

She shifted on the bench, turned her entire upper body toward him. "Look, I'm *not* mad. I'm...I'm *embarrassed*. I saw you and I just *assumed*...and then I all but ripped off your clothes, shoved you out on that runway."

"I could have stopped you at anytime, you know."

"Oh, really? And just when would that have been, Harry? While I was ripping open your shirt buttons, or maybe when I was on my knees, untying your shoes, yelling at you to drop your pants?"

"The name's Colin," he supplied carefully. He didn't want her to call him Harry. He wanted her to say his name, remember his name.

That adorable pointy chin went up. "I know that. Colin. Colin Rafferty. Max's cousin. Do you think that makes this any *better?*"

He grimaced. "Makes it even worse, huh? Yes, I suppose it does. I know Max isn't going to let me forget any of it for a long, long time. How about Julia?"

Holly shook her head. "She'll never bring it up again. She'll conveniently forget to show me the video. We're friends, and Julia never hurts a friend. Neither would Max."

"So that's good, right?" Colin persisted. "I get the blame, which I should, and the incident is forgotten. Right after you yell at me, call me names."

"Look, Har—Colin, I'm *not* going to yell at you. What good would that do? It was my mistake. Sure, you didn't make any effort to correct my mistake, but that doesn't mean the whole mess was your fault."

Colin gave in, tried on one of his best smiles, knowing she'd hate it…and went for the gold: "So we're agreed. I'm pretty much the innocent, injured party here. Basically the whole thing was your fault."

And we have lift-off…

Holly leapt to her feet, glared down at him. "My fault? *My* fault? How can you *say* that? What? You have no *mouth?* You couldn't say, 'Hey, lady, I'm not a male model, I'm Max's cousin'? You couldn't stop me—stop me at any time? You couldn't *keep your damn pants on?*"

"Uh-oh." Colin stood up, watching as a uniformed guard approached them with a determined look in his eyes. Colin knew he'd finally gotten the reaction he'd wanted from Holly, but maybe he should have waited until they were somewhere other than the very proper Frick to goad her into losing her cool.

He took her arm at the elbow and began maneuvering

her down the stone walkway. "Come on, little miss big mouth, before we're asked to leave."

"What?" Holly looked back over her shoulder, saw the guard, who was still moving toward them. "Oh, great. Oh, this is just *great*. It wasn't enough that you let me make an ass out of myself once—now you've gotten me to do it twice. I'll probably be barred from the museum after this."

"Yeah, well," Colin told her, all but frog-marching her at double-time toward the front door, her high heels *click-clicking* on the marble floor. "You know what they always say. See one *Storm Over Toledo* and you've seen them all."

She stopped dead, looked up at him...and then began to laugh. Colin would have grabbed her, hugged her, kissed her laughing mouth, but he was beginning to understand the meaning behind that old saying, "There's a time and place for everything." Because this wasn't it.

With the guard still in hot pursuit, Colin and Holly burst through the doorway and back out into the remarkably bright sunlight. Hand in hand, they trotted off down the pavement, not stopping until Holly grabbed at her side, the combination of their fast pace and her nearly uncontrollable giggling giving her the proverbial side-sticker.

"Wait...wait," she begged him, hanging on to his arm with both of hers. "You'll...you'll have to leave me behind, go on without me. I'm just slowing you down. Just...just be sure you deliver the secret plans to headquarters and...and remember me when you look into the eyes of your grandchildren."

Colin wrapped his arms around her, holding her close, and they both laughed until he became uncomfortably aware of the fact that his body was enjoying this mad little interlude more than he would have expected.

He took hold of her shoulders, pushed her slightly, safely, away from him, smiled down into her face. "Friends again?" he asked as she wiped tears of laughter from her cheeks, her "poor me" mood definitely a thing of the past.

"Maybe."

Making a quick decision, he took the opportunity to clear up any other misunderstandings they might have, so that they could start off with a clean slate. "So we're clear here? You know I'm sorry for letting you think I was someone I'm not."

"I think you're sorry now, but you weren't yesterday," Holly answered, clearly showing him that she knew him a little better than he'd expected, understood him a little more than might be comfortable.

God, she was everything he'd ever wanted, even when he hadn't known what he wanted. Smart, beautiful, totally unimpressed with his damn pretty face. Mercurial, soft hearted—she had just about dragged him into that restaurant yesterday, to feed him—with a wicked sense of humor.

Where had this remarkable woman been all his life? And, now that he'd found her, wasn't it just as remarkable that he was actually worried whether or not he could *keep* her? Him, Colin Rafferty, the guy who could get any girl he wanted, wanted a woman who just might not want him.

"And I'm not hypoglycemic," he added, hoping complete honesty would win the day for him.

Her eyelids narrowed over those now cloudy green eyes that reflected her every mood, every nuance of every mood. "If you're trying to remind me that I'm also gullible, believe everything people tell me, I think you've made your point. Now, is there anything else? Are those really your teeth? Are you wearing blue contacts over brown eyes? I know you don't have a wooden leg, but after what you pulled yesterday, I'd like to think I'm finally looking at the genuine Colin Rafferty."

"This is all me," Colin said, spreading his arms. "My own teeth, my real eye color, my very own hair weave."

Her eyes opened wide. "You have a hair weave? You're kidding! You actually have a hair weave? But it looks so natural. I never would have...wait a minute."

He raised his eyebrows, looked at her, waited, watched as the color invaded her cheeks.

"Oh, you bum! You don't have a hair weave. You just said that to see how I'd react. As if it would matter. Do you really think I'm that shallow?"

"No, I really think I get a kick out of watching your mood meter go up and down. I came after you to grovel—Max's suggestion was that I grovel—but I'm having a lot more fun this way. It's probably a good thing I threw the flowers in the trash."

"You brought me flowers? What kind?"

"I don't know. Yellow ones."

"And you threw them in the trash? Where?"

"Back there, at the Frick," Colin told her, then

grinned. "Do you want to go back and get them? I'll cover you, keep the guard busy while you grab them out of the trash."

"No, thanks," Holly said, walking across the wide sidewalk to a vendor cart near the curb. "If I'm going to start a life of crime, I'd rather bash you again with my purse. Right after you buy me a hot dog. Or maybe you've forgotten that we were supposed to be having lunch at Julia's right about now. I'm hypoglycemic, you know." She held out one hand. "Look, I'm shaking. My goodness, I could pass out at any moment."

"You don't give up easy, do you?" Colin asked, fishing in his pocket for some loose bills, then ordering hot dogs for both of them, sans onions. "I suppose you're going to keep bringing up every little mistake I've made since we met yesterday for the rest of our lives. Say it was your fault, then turn the screws a little about how, just maybe, it was my fault. My fault that you thought I was a male model, my fault that there really wasn't a right time yesterday to explain that I wasn't. My fault I don't have hypoglycemia, my fault you got chased out of the Frick—my fault we missed lunch at Julia's. Anything else?"

Holly pointed to the water bottles sitting in chipped ice on the food cart and raised two fingers at the vendor, who handed her two bottles. Then she looked at Colin. "Just one thing. What's this *for the rest of our lives* business?"

Colin handed her the hot dog in exchange for one of the water bottles, hoping she didn't decide to hit him with hers five seconds from now. "Oh? Didn't I tell you? Well, I guess there is just one more thing you're probably going to bring up from time to time over the years, so maybe I should have mentioned it sooner. You see, I've given it some thought, and I've decided that I'm going to marry you.''

Okay, Colin acknowledged to himself as he pounded on Holly's back until she could breathe again, so there were *two* things he probably should have said to her sooner. One, he was going to marry her and, two, "Maybe you shouldn't take a bite out of that hot dog until I tell you number one.''

Chapter Five

Holly looked askance at the Caller ID box, then reluctantly answered the ringing phone, hoping against hope that Colin Rafferty wasn't calling her from Julia's condo.

She could just let the answering machine pick up, but that would be cowardly. She'd rather be sneaky. Besides, if it was Colin Rafferty, boy, did she have a few choice things to say to that man! *"Sutherland,"* she purred into the receiver. "Sorry, the offices are closed right now, but if you wish to leave a message just wait for the tone and then speak slowly and distinctly—"

"Holly? Is that you?" Julia asked over the wires. "Thank goodness I found you. You weren't at the hotel, you weren't at your apartment. What are you doing in Allentown? I thought you weren't going back until tomorrow. Imagine how surprised I was when the desk clerk at the Waldorf told me you'd checked out. And without telling me."

"Sorry, Julia, I should have told you, but I was in a bit of a hurry to get out of the city before rush hour. I hate all that traffic in the tunnel, even if I'm not the one behind the wheel." Sitting back in her chair, looking at the clock on her desktop, Holly added, "I just changed my mind and came back tonight. We've got faxes, faxes and more faxes here, Julia, so it's a good thing I did. Somebody has to sort them out, get these orders moving."

"At nine o'clock at night? I don't think I pay you that well. Not after the three days you just put in for me in New York."

Holly was still looking at her clock. "Nine-oh-seven, if we're synchronizing our watches. And you pay me very well, thank you," she told her friend.

"I'm glad you think so, because I'm not giving you overtime to work yourself into a frazzle. Go home, Holly. Really, you need to go home."

"Look, Julia, it's okay. Irene is still at the Waldorf, packing up the gowns, doing everything she does so well, which left me free to come back here to start work on the postshow orders at this end, among other things. Or are you forgetting that there's a full line of Sutherland to watch over, on top of the bridal wear? So, is that it? Because I've got a desk piled high with work I have to get to tonight before I can finally go home."

"I don't know. Is there something else, Holly? You sound sort of huffy," Julia said after a slight pause. "You *are* huffy, aren't you? Why? Why are you in a huff, Holly? What did Colin do?"

Holly rolled her eyes. "Colin didn't do anything, Julia. I saw him this afternoon, he apologized. End of story."

"I don't believe you. There has to be more to it than that."

"Honestly, Julia, do you have to see secrets and drama in everything?"

"I see secrets, Holly," Julia pointed out calmly. "*You* see opportunities for drama. And there's nothing in any of those faxes, or piled on your desk, that couldn't have waited until tomorrow. We make clothing, Holly, we aren't milkmen, or florists. Our stock won't perish if it sits around one single extra day. Oh, and speaking of florists—did Colin bring you flowers? We told him to bring you flowers."

"Milk persons," Holly corrected Julia, because it was easier than answering Julia. "Milkman is politically incorrect in our highly evolved society. It might even be dairy product delivery persons."

"Well, consider me corrected. Now, did he bring you flowers? Because, after he left, I thought that maybe that wouldn't really be a good idea, since Richard was always bringing you flowers, and look how that ended up."

Holly pushed the palm of one hand against her head. "He didn't bring me flowers," she said, sighing. "Julia, I'm really busy here…"

"He didn't? Goodness, that's rather depressing. I wouldn't have thought he'd show up empty-handed. Not after that fiasco at the showing and after the way you stormed out of here when you saw him again. Didn't he bring you *anything?*"

"He bought me a hot dog from a vendor down the

street from the Frick,'' Holly said, sighing, blinking back sudden tears. How she hated to cry, which was unfortunate, since she had always been a world champion crier. At sad movies, at really good baby products commercials, at old songs playing on the radio. At backhanded, even high-handed, marriage proposals. Especially at them. Definitely.

"Oh, well, he bought you a hot dog. That changes everything, makes it all better,'' Julia was saying, and Holly could hear the smile in her friend's voice. "For me, roses, red ones. But for you? Food is perfect, just perfect. Especially junk food. I didn't know Colin was that perceptive. Did you cry? I'll bet you cried.''

"No, I did not cry,'' Holly singsonged, sitting up straight in her soft leather chair, the one chair she'd finally found at a local office supply store that let her feet actually reach the floor. "I thanked him, I ate the hot dog and then I came back to Allentown. Are we done now?''

"I'm done with you, yes,'' Julia said, her voice velvety soft, almost succeeding in hiding the sledgehammer she had wrapped inside it. "But I do know Colin's number at the Waldorf. Bye now.''

"No! Wait! Don't hang up!'' Holly jumped to her feet at this barely veiled attempt at blackmail, or coercion, or whatever it was—because, whatever it was, Julia Sutherland Rafferty was very, very good at it. "You wouldn't dare!''

"Aha! So there *is* something else. I knew it, I just knew it. Or did you think I can't tell when you're in one of your poor little Holly moods? You didn't rush back to Allentown without saying goodbye to me because you needed to go to work, Holly. You *ran* back to Allentown to get away from Colin. Come on, Holly, tell me. Spill your guts. You know you're going to tell me sooner or later, so why don't we just skip the middle, where you keep saying no, and go right to the end, where you tell me yes. Yes?''

Holly hit the button putting the phone on Speaker and hung up the receiver as she stood up, began to pace. "You're not going to let this go, are you?"

"That's a rhetorical question, right?" Julia responded, and now Holly could hear the laughter in her friend's voice. "Start at the beginning and tell me everything. Max is out, at a meeting with a vice president who just flew in from the plant in Phoenix, and the baby is in bed for the night. I have a pot of tea, some lovely warm scones to munch on and all the time in the world to listen."

Holly decided to cut to the chase. After all, she knew she was going to have to tell Julia sooner or later. This way, sooner, might just be less painful. "He said he thinks—he's pretty sure, actually, that he's going to marry me." She all but moaned the words as she shoved both hands through her already spiky hair. And she wasn't being overly dramatic, or in a mood, damn it. The man said he was going to marry her. What kind of crazy, dumb statement was that?

"What? What did you say? Holly, your voice sounds all hollow. Did you put me on the speaker? I hate being put on the speaker."

"I said, he said he's going to marry me," Holly repeated, slapping both palms on the desktop and leaning toward the phone. "Did you hear me now?"

Silly question. Obviously Julia had heard her, because what Holly heard next was some coughing, a few gasps, and then some more coughs. "Sorry," Julia said after a moment. "I was taking a sip of tea, and it went down wrong."

"Yeah, there's a lot of that going around," Holly said, still leaning on the desk top.

"What? Oh, never mind. I'm all right now. He said...he said he's going to *marry* you?" Julia asked. "When did he say that?"

"When? Don't you mean *why?*"

"Well, yes, that too, I suppose, except that Colin is Max's cousin, and the Raffertys are pretty well-known for making up their minds in a hurry, then doing everything in their power to—oh, brother. Holly, sweetie, brace yourself. I think you're in for a siege."

Holly had a quick flash back to Max's dogged pursuit of Julia once he'd reentered her life, determined to get her back, win her love once more. "Julia, this is different. Colin isn't Max, and Colin and I aren't married. You and Max were. This is just different. Besides, he was only teasing. We were both teasing—once I got done being so upset. He didn't really mean it. He couldn't have meant it."

"Which explains why you're back in Allentown?"

Wasn't it just like Julia to confuse everything with facts? "That also has nothing to do with anything. Look, you had to be there, okay? We were just fooling around. We were chased out of the Frick for making too much noise, and then we were cracking jokes, buying hot dogs. It was just something silly he said. Impulsive, spur-of-the-moment. It didn't mean a thing. I mean, he was buying me a hot dog at the time. How serious could that be?''

"Okay, I'm convinced," Julia teased. "Now convince yourself, because you don't sound convinced. And tell me, what did you do after he said he was going to marry you? Did you laugh? Did you both have a good laugh?''

Holly wished that's what they'd done. Instead, after horking up a bit of hot dog—such an elegant, romantic sight for Colin to witness—she'd run from him as if he'd just threatened her with a knife or something. She'd jumped into a cab, and raced back to the Waldorf to pack, to call for a limousine, to escape to the safety of Allentown.

"Laugh? Oh, yeah, sure. We both laughed," Holly said, hoping the distortion of the speakerphone would cover the fact that she was lying through her teeth. "He's quite a card, your husband's cousin. But we're fine now, both of us. He apologized, I accepted, we had a few laughs and we're fine now.''

"Cross your heart?''

"Cross my heart," Holly agreed rather fervently. "So now can I please go organize these faxes and check my phone messages before I go home and feed my goldfish? Helen's Joey was supposed to come feed them, but I'm sure he forgot. They're probably starving. You have no idea how guilty a goldfish's glare can make a person feel.''

"Certainly," Julia said, her tone so sweet, so satisfied, that Holly felt the hairs on the back of her head begin to prickle. "I'm completely satisfied now, and absolutely not worried a bit that Colin stopped by here earlier, asking directions to Allentown in general, to your apartment in particular. Good night, Holly, don't stay at the office too long. Because, as I believe I said earlier, you really, *really* should go home now.''

Holly stood very still for a long time, then slapped at the phone to cut off the dial tone that buzzed through the office like a swarm of angry bees. ''You're a rat, Julia Rafferty,'' she said to the dead air. ''A dirty, stinking, nosy *rat*.''

Then it hit her, really hit her. Here? He was coming here? Colin Rafferty was coming *here? When* was he coming here? *Why* was he coming here?

And where was *here?* Here, Allentown…or here, this office. Her office. Where she was now. Right now. Where she maybe shouldn't be right now if she was smart. Because maybe she should be at home, in her apartment. But if she was there, she'd have to barricade the door, because Colin might be coming to her apartment, and what would she do if he showed up at her apartment? If he showed up here? If he showed up, period?

Holly closed her eyes, took three deep, steadying breaths. ''Okay, now that you've panicked,'' she told herself, ''it's time to slow down, calm down, think like a rational adult. You can do this, Holly.''

She closed her eyes, drew her breath in on a not quite silent sob. ''No, you can't. You cannot handle Colin Rafferty. You don't even *want* to handle Colin Rafferty.''

She winced. ''Okay, so maybe you do want to handle Colin Rafferty, but that's neither here nor there, and probably X-rated, so just forget it, okay? And think. Think!''

What she thought was that she had passed beyond the "drama" Julia had talked about, heading straight for melodrama. She had to stop that, stop that now. She could not afford to indulge herself in one of her flights of fancy, one of her interior scenarios that were so often built around her extremely overactive imagination, her ability—or curse—that allowed her to go to extremes with the speed of a sports car going from zero to sixty in mere seconds.

Colin was coming to Allentown, might already be in the city. Might already be camped on her doorstep, waiting for her, lying in wait for her.

She, Holly Hollis, extremely unexceptionable short person, was being hotly pursued by a Greek god who said he wanted to marry her.

And this was a bad thing?

How was this a *bad* thing?

"Oh, let me count the ways," Holly moaned, collapsing once more into her desk chair.

One, the man was gorgeous, and she'd sworn off gorgeous, even if Colin wasn't a male model. He was still prettier than she was, and who wanted to go through life feeling like she should know darn full well that, hey, the two of them were *not* a matched set?

Two, he was Max's cousin. What if they did date, did get serious about each other and then broke up? What if they got married, and then divorced? How could she continue on with Julia, Max's wife, if suddenly they were "family," and then, just as suddenly, they weren't?

Three, he was nuts. She had to consider that. Definitely. Because only a nut would propose—sort of propose—to a woman he'd known less than twenty-four hours. Right?

Four, she couldn't let him meet her family. Dear God, her mother would have a conniption! She'd take one look at Colin and start waxing poetic over having the most beautiful grandchildren in the history of grandchildren. She'd meet Colin a single time, have him in her house a single time, for Sunday dinner or something, and the whole time she'd grill Holly hourly about "How's it going, dear?" until Holly ran screaming from the room. Except she couldn't run screaming from the room because then her mother would only turn to Colin and ask, "So, how's it going, dear?"

Five, and most important, Holly wasn't about to let her heart get broken again. Not that Richard had exactly broken her heart, but he'd definitely bruised it, bent it, left it and her self-esteem sort of scuffed and walked-on. Richard had been big on "I love you." Real big on "I love you." Said it all the time. She just hadn't realized that he'd probably been addressing his reflection in her gullible eyes.

Holly couldn't trust a man who said "I love you" so glibly, said, "I'm going to marry you" so glibly. Who would?

Unfortunately she would, and had…because she'd believed Richard for a while, at least for a little while. But that didn't mean she was going to trust another pretty face mouthing pretty words.

Not in this lifetime! Once bitten, twice shy, and all that good stuff that was so trite, yet so true. That's what

Holly was, twice shy, and what she would wisely continue to be—and Colin Rafferty wouldn't stand a chance.

Not if he camped on her doorstep, brought her dozens of yellow flowers, smiled that kneecap-melting smile of his that went right up to his eyes. Not if he said silly, outrageous things to her. Not if he wooed her and chased her from now until the end of time.

Yeah, sure. He'd chase her all right. About as long as Richard had chased her. Handsome men didn't have to waste their time chasing after women who didn't want them; they were too busy either running from women who did, or allowing themselves to be caught.

None of which, of course, really explained why Colin Rafferty had asked Julia for directions to Allentown, to Holly's apartment.

Holly got up and walked over to switch on the lights inside the large fitting area, an area equipped with several floor-to-ceiling mirrors. She stepped up on the platform positioned in front of a trio of those mirrors, and tipped her head to one side as she examined her triple reflection, looking for clues.

Nothing. There was nothing reflected in any of the mirrors that would have made her look irresistible to Colin Rafferty. Hair, spiky. Face, holding up well, considering she was zeroing in on her twenty-ninth birthday. Body, short. Curved in the right places, granted, but short.

Nope, nothing. This was not a face or body that would launch a thousand ships. Maybe a canoe—on a good day, a tugboat—but not a thousand ships.

So what about her had appealed to him? She knew

now what had appealed to Richard. He'd fallen in love with her connection to Sutherland, plain and simple.

But Colin didn't need *connections*. He was Colin Rafferty. He was a big cog in the huge wheel of Majestic Enterprises, Max's company. The man had lived in Paris, for crying out loud, home of more beautiful women than most any other city in the world. The saying was "How ya gonna keep 'em down on the farm after they've seen Paree." Not, "See Holly Hollis and forget Paris."

"I'm a challenge," she decided at last, hopping down from the platform and heading back to her office. "That's it, plain and simple. I didn't go gaga over him, fall all over him because he's so gorgeous, turn on my back and wag my tail like some pathetic puppy, hoping he'd scratch my belly. In fact, I told him I was turned off by his good looks. Man, I'll bet he hasn't heard that one before! So now he thinks he's interested, just because I'm not."

She shook her head as she picked up her purse, walked over to punch in the security code. "Sure. I'm not interested. Not a bit. Hollis, lie to Julia. Lie to the whole world. But don't lie to yourself."

Her hand halted in midair, poised in front of the alarm control panel. "Keep trying to get rid of him, and the more he'll want to stay. Simple psychology." She closed her eyes, made a face. "No, I can't do that. It would be mean. Not fair, or even honest, since I do sort of like the idea of having him around. Still, it could be interesting…"

Colin arched his back against the soft leather seat of his rented BMW, trying to ease his discomfort after a nearly three-hour drive in heavy traffic and two hours spent sitting in the parking lot of Holly's apartment building, waiting for her to come home.

Had he always been this impulsive? He didn't think so. Yet here he was, checked out of his suite at the Waldorf, his luggage locked in the trunk of the BMW, with no hotel reservations and no idea what he'd say to Holly if and when she finally showed up.

Irene had given him a few helpful hints, when he'd run down that good woman at the Waldorf. Don't be too pushy, Irene had told him, but don't give her too much time to think, either. Don't flatter her a lot, because she won't believe you. Do bring her food, because Holly loves to eat. Consider jellybeans, the red ones most especially.

"Oh," Irene had added, "and you might want to think about looking less like the cover model on *GQ*, if you can figure out a way to manage that. That could only help matters. Lastly, you'd better be telling me the truth, young man, because if you hurt that little girl I'm going to have to hurt you."

Colin smiled now, remembering the stern look on Irene's face as she'd given him her warning. It would seem that Julia hadn't just built a successful company; she'd built a family from her employees. That was nice, and very like the atmosphere Max tried to foster throughout the sprawling Majestic Enterprises. Big shouldn't mean impersonal, that's what Max had told him, and so far, Max had made it work.

Max made a lot of things work, and Colin knew he could have done a lot worse in choosing a role model.

But his admiration for Max, as a cousin, as an employer, as a man, only went so far. It did not extend to include listening to that man's advice given late this afternoon over cocktails at the Waldorf bar.

"A full-out assault on her mind and heart," Max had instructed him. "Move in, take over, make it impossible for her to ignore you. Don't give her time to think. You two are perfect for each other, but she's not going to believe that, not if you give her time to think. Be romantic, Colin. You do know how to be romantic, don't you?"

Yes, Colin knew how to be romantic. But, he'd decided, with Holly, it would probably be better to go with the jellybeans.

He was sitting low on his spine in the leather seat, fighting the heaviness in his eyelids, trying not to fall asleep as the clock on the dash displayed the fact that it was nearly nine-thirty. He was still operating on Paris time, and his body wasn't sure if it was sleepy, awake, or even hungry.

Was that it? Maybe he wasn't thinking clearly. Maybe that's why he'd gotten it into his head that Holly Hollis was the one woman in the world he wanted, would always want.

Love by jet lag?

Anything was possible.

Except that he still didn't know if he loved her. How could he know that? He wasn't a complete fool, he was more than a little aware that what he felt for Holly Hollis could be infatuation, physical attraction, the thrill of not being pursued solely because of his physical appearance.

Except that it didn't feel like something so simple as physical attraction, or even the considerable challenge she presented by running away from him each time he tried to get closer to her.

There was more to it than that. He didn't know just what, couldn't put a name to it or describe it, but there was just some *something* about Holly that made him want to protect her, tease her, excite her, make her laugh, get her to talk to him again as honestly as they had spoken last night.

So where did this "I'm going to marry you" stuff come from? He'd said it. He'd heard himself say it. But where had it come from? What insane part of him had blurted out that sort of declaration on a city street in Manhattan—while buying hot dogs, for crying out loud?

That was probably the jet lag part of this whole deal. It was the only explanation.

Nothing, however, explained what he was doing here now, skulking down in his seat to keep his head out of sight, waiting for Holly to come home.

If he was smart, he'd call it a night. Find himself a motel somewhere back along the highway, pack it in for the night and make a fresh start in the morning. When he was rested. Clearheaded. Reasonably sane.

Deciding he'd at last discovered at least one right thing to do, Colin sat up, reached toward the ignition, just as headlights appeared and a car turned into the parking lot. Scratch that, not a car. A ragtop 4x4. He knew—he didn't know how he knew—but he knew, and would bet a considerable sum, that Holly was behind the wheel.

Moments later, he was proven right. He watched as Holly opened the door on the driver's side, then aimed her size five feet at the macadam. He wondered if she'd chosen the 4x4 because it was compact, rather like her, or if it was the one car she could drive without using a booster seat.

Not that he'd ask her. He already knew she saw her petiteness as a sort of drawback, while he just loved how small she felt when he wrapped his arms around her, how strong and powerful he felt—the man, the protector, the big brave guy who hunted the meat, while she kept the cave warm. Or Sutherland's in great working order, which had to be the modern, liberated equivalent of "keeping the cave warm."

He continued watching as she dragged a huge suitcase out of the Jeep, followed by one smaller suitcase, then a folded garment bag, then a canvas sports-type bag that could conceivably hold a half-dozen basketballs. How long had she been in New York? Six months?

She set the large suitcase upright, pulled out the built-in handle, then worked the handle of the sports bag over it. The garment bag she slung over her left shoulder, while she gripped the smaller suitcase in her left hand.

Add that near-suitcase of a purse, and she was probably outweighed two-to-one by her luggage. Not that any such consideration stopped her. Oh, no, not Holly. She just bent her head and sort of hunched her shoulders and back, having some trouble starting from her standing stop, and slowly began to move forward.

Colin quietly exited his sports car, carefully closing the door behind him so that it made little noise. He walked across the parking lot, arriving at the curb just as Holly was calling that strip of cement some rather unlovely names as she struggled to pull the wheeled luggage up and over the barrier.

"Don't blame the curb for being there, Holly," he said, standing behind her. "Haven't the words *two trips* ever entered your vocabulary?"

She didn't even flinch. No shriek of surprise, or shock. No looking back over her shoulder. No outraged, "What are you doing here!"

She just let go of the handle on the largest suitcase and said, "I was wondering if you were going to just stand back and watch while I struggled with this mess. It's nice to know you're at least a semigentleman. Now grab those two and follow me, okay?"

Colin stood there for a moment, then shook his head. "Julia. She told you, right?"

"And perceptive, too," Holly remarked to the night air, already on the move again. "Except that he's here when I so clearly don't want him here, which drops his IQ more than a few points."

The suitcase he was dragging hit a rock or something and began to tip, which shifted the sports bag, and suddenly he was busy trying to keep both upright. And all the while, Holly was walking ahead of him, keeping up that breakneck pace she was so good at. "Stupid invention. Oh, the hell with it," he said, picking up both bags and charging after her.

"Nice layout," he said as she stopped in front of a white metal door designed to look like a traditional six-panel wooden door. The complex was made up of a half-dozen redbrick buildings, each holding, he guessed, about a dozen units. The buildings had been constructed on a hillside, so that half the units had ground-floor entrances on one side, the actual second-floor units had similar "ground-floor" entrances on their side. Very inventive, actually. Each unit also had its own front door, its own small patio. Holly's unit was actually a second floor unit, and her particular patio sported a small, two-person wooden glider and was lined with black pots holding red and white geraniums.

"Thanks. It's humble, but it's home," Holly said, still fishing in her huge purse for her keys, which she'd thrown in there while gathering up her ton of luggage. "*My* home. You're not invited."

He ignored her bad humor, rather enjoyed it as a matter of fact, because she tried so hard to be unreasonable. Teasing her out of her bad moods could become his life's work, as a matter of fact. "Yes, I rather sensed that. But do you tip? Two dollars a bag is customary."

"In your dreams," Holly responded, finally locating the key ring and opening the front door. She turned, looked at him. "Oh, come on. Don't just stand there like some stray dog expecting to be fed. It's disgusting."

She turned on a few lights from the switch beside the front door, then dropped her two pieces of luggage on the small tiled area that served as a foyer. "Just leave them there for now. I'm too tired to even think about unpacking tonight."

He gratefully dropped the bags—what had she packed in them anyway? Cannonballs?—and followed her into the spacious living room.

He'd spent the last three years living in the Majestic

Enterprises corporate apartment. Formal. Fancy. Almost rigid. This room was anything but rigid. The walls were painted a deep, forest-green, the berber carpet was nearly white. The tables were big, which they had to be, to hold all the family photographs Holly had piled on them. The couches, both of them, were covered in some sort of country-type print splashed all over with colorful flowers, then nearly smothered with pillows.

There was an old-fashioned rocker in one corner, occupied by three plush teddy bears. The lamps on either side of the larger couch had Tiffany shades, so that jewel colors reflected on the ceiling when she turned them on. A small aquarium stood on its own stand near the front window, bubbling merrily, stocked with colorful goldfish Holly was now feeding.

There were art prints on the walls, about a dozen plants scattered here and there—all of them good fakes, he was pretty sure, because Holly would hate to kill anything, even a philodendron, and she was often away from home—and a half-dozen thick ivory candles on the coffee table.

And, lastly, there was a popcorn machine in the corner of the L-shaped area that served as a dining room. An honest-to-God, commercial-size popcorn maker.

"It's perfect," he said, shaking his head as he walked over to inspect the bright red-and-yellow machine. "Everything is exactly what I would have said you'd have in your home. Although the popcorn maker is probably a stretch. I'll admit it, I might have missed that one."

"My brother—Herb, not Harry—is a projectionist at one of the local multiplexes. They were replacing the popcorn machine, and he grabbed it for me. It was a Christmas present."

"Of course it was," Colin said, heading for the kitchen, which he could see from the dining room.

"He was batting a thousand with me, too," she continued, closing the top on the fish food and following after him. "Until he gave me the aquarium for my birthday. What do I want with goldfish? I hate having a pet. I don't need the responsibility."

Colin raised one eyebrow at this statement. For a girl surrounded by a loving family, she sure went out of her way to avoid any sort of emotional involvement.

Who was she trying to fool? She craved emotional involvement. It was being hurt that she did her damnedest to avoid. Even flushing a goldfish would probably break her heart—and he'd bet she'd hold a small funeral, hum taps, the whole nine yards. "The phone's in here?"

Holly nodded, pointing to the unit on the wall beside the refrigerator. "Why? You need to make a call? Maybe to Information, for the name of the nearest motel? Hey, be my guest."

"Actually," he said, lifting the receiver and pushing a single button, "I'm calling for pizza. I had a feeling you'd have the number for one already listed on your speed dial. Plain or pepperoni?"

She narrowed her eyelids for a moment and glared at him, then relented. "Plain, extra cheese. Only because I forgot to eat dinner. And I don't like you. I don't like you one little bit."

"I know," Colin said. "Isn't this fun?"

She raised both hands, closed them into fists, then sort of growled before turning on her heels and leaving the kitchen.

Chapter Six

This wasn't going well. Holly was finding it more and more difficult to act like a jerk, even if she still felt like a jerk. She'd been rude, she'd told him she didn't like him.

Nothing fazed him. He just kept coming back for more, smiling, being so darn *nice,* and even as she redoubled her efforts to stay in a bad mood, she just couldn't seem to maintain her frown in the face of his smile. That in itself was an accomplishment she couldn't understand. Nobody had *ever* been able to snap her out of one of her bad moods but herself. Yet Colin was doing it, with ease.

"Are you sure you don't want me to carry your luggage into your bedroom?" Colin asked now, having returned to the living room after phoning for the pizza delivery.

"Oh, all right," she said, trying to sound as if his polite offer annoyed her past all endurance. "I might as well put you to work, as long as you're here. And why are you here, anyway?''

"I couldn't help myself," Colin said with an eyebrow-waggling grin. He picked up the same two bags he'd carried into the apartment as she grabbed the other two, then followed her down the hall toward the larger of the two bedrooms in the apartment. But he stopped in front of the open door to the smaller bedroom. "What's this? A home office?"

"No, it's not a home office. I'm at the office enough, thank you, without bringing it home with me. Come on, my bedroom is this way."

"Oh, is that ever a line a man could get used to hearing," he said, and she hid a reluctant smile and started off again, then stopped, because she sensed that he wasn't following her.

"Hey!" she said, truly angry now, because he'd put down the luggage and had stepped inside the smaller bedroom, flipped on the wall switch that turned on the overhead light. "That's off limits."

She was about to retrace her steps down the hall when he emerged from the room, holding her acoustic guitar. "You play?" he asked, rather carelessly holding the guitar by the neck, making her wince.

"Give me that," she commanded, dropping her bags and aiming herself toward the guitar. Colin quickly raised his arm above his head, effectively putting the guitar out of her reach. "Very funny," she growled at him. "And, no, I am *not* going to jump up and down like some idiot, trying to grab the guitar. I stopped doing that years ago, when I figured out it doesn't work. So I'll give you to the count of three, then do what I did to my brothers and anyone else who ever tried this trick on me—I'll kick you square in the shins.''

He grinned at her. ''Figures. Women rarely play fair.''

''Play fair?'' Holly pointed up at the guitar, still held above his head. ''You call what you're doing playing *fair?*''

''Point taken.'' He lowered the guitar, which she immediately grabbed out of his hand. ''So, do you play?''

''No,'' she grumbled, carrying the guitar back into the room, replacing it in the corner, ''I just keep it around because that way nosy people can go poking around my apartment, uninvited, and *ask* me if I play.''

She stomped back down the hall, picked up the small suitcase and garment bag, and completed her trip into her bedroom, Colin once more close behind her. ''There,'' she said, pointing toward the empty space beneath the window. ''Put them there…please.''

''Nice room,'' he said as he deposited the bags, then put his hands on his hips, looking around the room as if he contemplated moving in—which would happen only in his dreams, or hers. ''Where's the stepladder so you can get into that bed?''

Holly felt herself blushing. ''It's called a rice bed,'' she said, looking at the huge, queen-size cherry four-poster, complete with canopy. ''I've always wanted one, but it didn't occur to me how *high* it would be when topped with a good box spring and a pillow-top mattress. I have a matching step stool for it, on the other side of the bed.''

''So when you say you climb into bed at night, you literally do *climb* into bed at night,'' Colin said, that same wonderful smile attacking her again, making her very aware that the two of them were standing in her bedroom.

"Sometimes," Holly admitted, trying to keep the conversation light until she could somehow get past Colin and head back toward the living room. "Sometimes I just get a running start and jump up on it."

"I'd like to see that," Colin said. "Although I suppose you've never tried it with a pole vault? That could be fun."

"Nope. I've never, and you won't." Holly took a breath, tried to make herself even smaller, skinnier, and quickly brushed past him, heading for the safety of the living room. She flopped down on the smaller of the matching couches, and curled her legs up under her, then tossed a pile of pillows onto the other cushion, so that Colin couldn't sit down beside her.

"Good," he said as he entered the living room. "You stay there, put your feet up, rest. I'll scrounge around in the kitchen, find us glasses, plates, napkins. The pizza should be here soon."

Holly scrambled off the couch and raced ahead of him, into the kitchen. "No need," she said, knowing she looked silly, standing, arms spread wide, in front of the cabinets. It was just that he was invading every corner of her life. Her living room, her bedroom—and she had to draw a line somewhere or else have to move out of the apartment once he was gone, to banish the memory of him in it. "You just go sit down, and I'll get everything. Do you want crushed hot peppers? Garlic powder?"

"Definitely not garlic powder, unless you're planning

on some," he told her, once more setting her emotions off on a roller-coaster ride to confusion. "Ah, there goes the doorbell. I'll be right back."

"Wait! I…I'll pay for the pizza," Holly said, remembering that he was a guest—uninvited, but still a guest—in her home.

"You can pay me back," Colin said, already heading toward the front door. "But I warn you, I'm a big tipper."

Holly grumbled under her breath and went about assembling plates, knives and forks—in case he was one of those weirdos, who thought pizza should be eaten that way. Her favorite pizza cutter, because the pizzas never were cut all the way through. Napkins were already on the small round table in the dining room. She grabbed condiments from the slim closet next to the stove, snared two cans of cola from the fridge and met Colin in the dining room.

He set the cardboard box in the middle of the table and flipped it open. "Oh, would you look at that. A thing of beauty and a joy until it's gone. You wouldn't want Parisian pizza, Holly." He deftly employed the pizza slicer, using swift, economical motions of his hand to roll the cutter through the pie as he deftly turned the box. A real pro. "Personally I think the guy who invented no sauce pizza, broccoli pizza and all those other nonpizzas, should be banned from ever being within fifty yards of a pizza shop."

Holly agreed. "And what's with all these new kinds of pizza, anyway?" she asked, holding up her plate so that Colin could slide a slice onto it. "Cheese in the crust? Two crusts? Upside-down pizza, or whatever?

Me, if I can't fold a slice in half and watch while oil drips off it onto the plate, it *ain't* pizza."

"Ah, a woman after my own heart. I'll bet that's upsetting the hell out of you, that we have so much in common. But it's decision time, Holly. Crushed peppers?" Colin asked, holding up the small glass jar. "Garlic powder?" he asked, holding that jar in his other hand.

Holly looked at both containers, knowing defeat when she stared it in the face, then quickly reached for the crushed peppers.

"Yes, progress," Colin said rather smugly as he slid a slice onto his own plate, then sat down. "Would you like me to tell you about the two summers I spent as head dough thrower at a pizza parlor in Ocean City?"

"New Jersey or Maryland?" Holly asked him, trying not to sound too interested.

"The Jersey shore," he said, sprinkling a generous amount of crushed red pepper on top of the bubbled cheese. "I attended college at Princeton, so the shore was a natural place to spend my summers, considering Mom and Dad were off somewhere, digging up pots and hooking prize trout."

"Wasn't that difficult? Not seeing your parents, I mean?" Holly surprised herself with that question, considering the fact that she certainly had been heard to complain that her own family sometimes smothered her with attention.

"Oh, I saw them. Just not at the same time, and not at home—if I could remember where we were living at the time. Mom came to lecture at Princeton a couple of times, and Dad entered a few sport fishing contests, then dropped by to see how his boy was doing. And I had Max's parents, Max, plenty of friends. I got along.''

Holly reached for a second slice, sprinkled it with peppers. "I can't imagine it, being on my own so much. Oh, I mean, sure, I'm on my own. Figuratively. I have my job, I have this apartment, but I know I'm only fifteen minutes or a local phone call away from my family.''

''Family's important to you?''

She chewed on a mouthful of pizza as she chewed on his question. ''Yes, it is. I complain, I wish they'd keep their noses out of my business, but I can't imagine *not* having them around. The nieces and nephews dropping in unannounced, my sister calling to ask me to go along with her to the mall. Cookouts at my brothers' houses in the summer, renting videos and popping popcorn for a living room full of Hollises in the winter time. My dad stopping by to replace the washer in my kitchen sink, my mom calling to ask about my love—well, never mind.''

''I see. So, dropping everything and going to, say, Paris for three years, wouldn't appeal to you?''

Holly looked down at her plate, amazed to realize she'd suddenly lost her appetite. ''No,'' she said, slowly shaking her head. ''That wouldn't appeal to me. Not at all. I would have *thought* it would, but now that I really think about it? I'd never want to be more than about two hours or so away from my family. Gee,'' she ended, propping her chin on her hand as she balanced her elbow on the edge of the table, ''that's depressing, isn't it? I always thought I wanted to be a world traveler.''

''I have to go back to Paris next weekend,'' Colin

told her, then took a long drink from his can of cola.
"I doubt I'll be back in the States again until Christmas."

"Really?" Holly said, avoiding his intense, intent
gaze. "But that's all right for you, isn't it. I mean, it
hasn't bothered you so far, or you wouldn't be doing
it, right?"

"Right," Colin said, flipping the pizza box shut and
carrying it into the kitchen, sliding it into the refrigerator. "It never bothered me before."

Before? Before what? Holly wondered. Before he'd
come back to the States, realized he'd missed American
food? Before he'd met her? Before she'd lost her tiny
little mind?

He returned to the dining room and Holly quickly
stood up, began gathering plates and napkins before he
could do all the cleanup himself. It was definitely time
for a change of subject. "Tell me about being head
pizza tosser, or whatever it was you said."

His smile was so sweet, so suddenly boyish, that
Holly nearly had to grab on to the back of the chair to
keep from throwing herself into his arms. "It was a
blast," he said, helping her clear the table. "The shop
was open to the air, right on the boardwalk, and I stood
smack in front of the shop, tossing rounds of dough into
the air. There's an art to it, you know, involving me-
dium-level dexterity, and a lot of flour rubbed on your
hands and forearms. I worked the four to twelve shift,
and usually had a pretty good audience."

Holly threw the crumpled paper napkins into the trash
can kept behind the door of the cabinet beneath the sink,
and headed out of the kitchen, picking up her soda can

as she aimed herself toward the couch once more—this time the larger one.

"You really were one of those guys who threw the pizza into the air? We vacationed in Ocean City a few times, when I was still living at home. I can remember spending what seemed like hours, watching guys like you, watching other guys make fudge, or taffy. Although I'm betting a lot of your audience of teenage girls weren't watching the dough fly into the air."

"I had my share of admirers," Colin admitted, that heart-melting smile in evidence once more. "And I'm told that my finesse with the paddles—sliding the pizzas in and out of the brick oven—was poetry in motion. In other words, I had some memorable summers."

"I got bitten by a jellyfish one summer, and fell asleep on the beach another summer and got burned to a crisp. But the worst was going to the movies with the family, dressed in shorts, no makeup—and being handed a kiddie ticket. That hurts, when you're seventeen."

"I wish I could have seen you then," Colin said, sitting down beside her, the guitar in his hand. How had he done that? How had he slipped down the hall and grabbed her guitar without her noticing?

She pointed to the guitar. "I put that away. There's a reason I put that away, Colin."

He sat on the edge of the couch, the guitar balanced on one knee, the thick braided strap slung around his neck. "I'm sure there is," he agreed, then winced as he ran his thumb down the strings. "And there it is—this thing is *way* out of tune."

"That's because I don't play it," Holly told him,

feeling herself getting peevish. That was a good thing. She needed to be peevish, because she was liking this man entirely too much. And, according to her theory, if she showed that she liked him, if she appeared even slightly interested in him romantically, he'd run from her as if the hounds of hell were after him. "Now put it back, okay?"

"Why do you have it, if you don't play it?" Colin asked, working to adjust the strings, bring the guitar back into tune. He had his eyes closed, his head bent as he listened to each sound, made adjustments on those pegs or whatever they were called at the skinny end of the guitar.

He was strumming the guitar now, just running his hand over the strings, and the sound was so familiar, so haunting, that Holly could feel her chest tightening. "It was my grandfather's. He used to play it for me all the time. Mom...well, Mom said I could have it."

His head still bent over the strings, Colin turned his head, looked at her, his blue eyes soft, full of compassion. "Good memories, huh?"

Holly nodded. "Very good memories. Grandpop used to play, and I'd sing. Not well, but I was loud. He said it was one of the miracles of nature that such a big voice could be stuffed inside such a small body. But," she ended, sighing, "I never did learn how to play. Except for 'Pop Goes The Weasel.' I played one note in that one."

"'Pop Goes The Weasel,' huh?" Colin said, shifting slightly on the couch. "And I'll bet I know the note you played. Let's try it, okay?"

Holly nodded, then watched as Colin picked out the

simple tune on her grandfather's guitar. When it came
to the "Pop!" part of the song, he lifted his hands from
the strings and she reached over, plucked the proper
string, then sat back as he finished the chorus. Three
times, she reached over to pluck that single string, make
that musical "Pop!" and by the time the song was done,
tears were streaming down her cheeks.

"Hey, I'm sorry," Colin said, putting down the guitar as he reached for her, drew her into his arms. "I
didn't mean to make you cry."

"I'm not crying," Holly protested against his chest,
trying to sneakily lift a hand to her face to wipe away
her tears. "It's just…it's just that so many good memories of Grandpop just washed over me."

She pushed herself away from his chest, but he held
onto her arms, not letting her sit back against the cushions.

"You think I'm an idiot, don't you?" she asked him,
sniffling. "I try not to be so emotional, but I'm not very
good at it. Happy, sad, I just seem to *feel* everything.
But I could close my eyes while you were playing, and
just *see* myself sitting on the floor at Grandpop's knee,
trying to be still but just about jumping out of my skin,
waiting to pluck the string." She closed her eyes now.
"He always smelled so good, like shoe polish and pipe
tobacco, and he always had candy for me…"

Colin reached in his pocket and pulled out a snow-
white linen square, used it to wipe at the tears on
Holly's cheeks. "You're very lucky, Holly. One, to
have known your grandfather. My grandparents were all
gone by the time I was born. And, two, to be able to

feel the way you do. Not everybody can, you know. I think it's healthier. Feeling, that is."

Holly took the handkerchief from him, pressing it to her cheeks as she stood up, stepped away from the couch. "Excuse me," she said. "I'm going to go wash my face."

"Okay," Colin said, once more strumming the guitar, obviously understanding that, at least for now, the subject was closed.

She hated that he was so understanding, so *nice*. She hated that just having him here, in her living room, was doing things to her that probably could keep a shrink busy for months and months.

She was happy.

She was sad.

She was attracted.

She was angry.

She was confused.

She, if pressed, would probably have to say, "Wait a minute, let me think," if someone asked her her middle name.

"Marie," she said as she stomped down the hallway to her bedroom. "My middle name is Marie. And his middle name is mud, because I'm not going to let this guy get to me, then walk away, fly off to Paris, do whatever it is he's bound to do. I'm just not!"

That resolve, heartily meant, lasted until she'd washed her face free of makeup, tossed her slacks and sweater onto the bed and dressed in sweats and an old University of Pennsylvania sweatshirt, and opened the door to the hallway once more.

Because that's when she heard it. Colin was sitting

in her living room, expertly playing "Girl from Ipanema," and quietly singing the words in a voice that sounded like expensive scotch poured over velvet.

Was there *anything* this guy couldn't do?

She hung back in the hallway until the song was over, then flounced, barefoot, back into the living room and all but threw herself down on the couch. "It's late. You should go."

"You look terrific," he said, and she touched the tip of her nose, which she knew to be shiny.

"I look twelve," she countered, then helped the image along by pulling her legs up onto the couch, sitting there cross-legged, her hands on her knees. "Seriously, you have to go. I need to be at work really early tomorrow. You do have a hotel room, don't you? Or are you planning to drive all the way back to New York at this hour?"

"Nope, I'm not going back to New York. I'm here for the duration." He patted the couch cushion. "Is this a sleeper sofa by any chance?"

It was, because sometimes one of the nieces or nephews would come over, spend the night. "No, it's not. And, even if it was, you can't stay here."

"I can be harmless, Holly," he said, using that damn sexy smile on her again.

"Sure. So can hungry alligators," she countered. reaching for her soda can. "Seriously, Colin, you have to go."

"Because I scare you?" he asked, strumming the guitar strings again.

"No!" Holly exploded, hopping off the couch. "You

do *not* scare me. Although you should, because you're nuts, you know. Crazy. Wacko.''

"Wacko? Why? Because I said I'm going to marry you? Because I followed you here to Allentown and sat outside your door for hours, like some lovesick schoolboy?''

"All right, that's good for starters," Holly agreed, pacing in front of the coffee table like a caged lioness. "And why did you do that?" she asked, stopping, turning to point a finger at him. "Why?''

"Why did I say I'm going to marry you?''

"Yes, why did you say you're going to marry me. And stop smiling at me!''

Colin propped the guitar against the side of the couch, sat back, looked up at her. "To tell you the truth, Holly, I don't know why I said it. I just opened my mouth, and it came out. Shocked the hell out of me. I'm still trying to deal with it myself, which answers your second question, which is, why am I here.''

"And I thought I was the only one who'd gone crazy this week," Holly muttered under her breath. "Okay," she said then, "I'll help you. You've got a crush on me. Oh, yes, don't shake your head. You've got a crush on me. I know, because I've had crushes myself, although not since college, I will admit that. Except maybe for Richard, but we won't discuss him, either. But that's it—a crush. You probably never had one before, considering the fact that you've always been the one that was chased, not the one who had to do the chasing. And don't deny that one, because I wasn't born yesterday, you know.''

Colin shook his head. "I don't understand," he said,

beginning to rise from the couch, so that she stuck out her arm, motioning for him to stay where he was.

"A crush, Colin. A *crush*. An unexplainable, heart-pounding, stomach-flipping, I can't sleep or eat *crush*. A yearning for the unattainable, based on all kinds of things, none of them having anything to do with logic. A transitory madness, but one you'll get over, just to wake up one morning and say, 'My God, what was I *thinking?*'"

"And that's what's happening here? I have a crush on you? Interesting. So that's why all I want to do is kiss you until your toes curl up and you sigh into my mouth and melt against me, whisper my name over and over as I make love to you until we're both limp and spent and fall asleep in each other's arms—just so we can wake up and do it all again? Because I have a crush on you?"

Holly tried to swallow, couldn't. The man could inspire one hell of a mental picture. She looked down at her bare feet, appalled to see that she'd been curling her toes into the plush carpet. "Yeah, sure," she said, her voice rather broken. "That's it exactly. A crush. Maybe a little more…a bit more *advanced* than the sort of crushes I've had, but you've got the general idea. Believe me, it's transitory. It will go away as quickly as it came."

He stood up, somehow filling the room, making it difficult for her to breathe. "I don't think so. That it will go away, I mean. This crush is pretty intense."

Holly whimpered, struggled to get a grip on herself. "Look, Colin," she said, backing up until her calves were pressing against the facing couch. "Let me explain this to you in more detail, okay? We met, under rather…well, rather unusual circumstances.''

He nodded. ''All right. I'll concede that one. You in a boa, me without my pants.''

''Gee, thanks for the reminder,'' Holly said, allowing some sarcasm into her voice, because she really was operating under a strain here. ''Anyway, I was honest with you. *Too* honest. Blunt, even. I told you I'm not attracted to male models—translation, men so handsome they should be outlawed, or licensed, or something. Maybe come with warning labels. In other words, I told you, right up front, that there was no way—no way—there could ever be anything between us.''

''Yes, you did make that rather clear.''

''Thank you, I tried,'' Holly said, his bland expression and careful attendance to what she was saying coming very close to pressing her Giggle button. The man really was something else. Good-looking—great-looking—and with a sense of humor, a love of the ridiculous. From his Tom Cruise eyebrows to the way he attacked a hot pizza, there was nothing about him that didn't appeal to her.

Which was why she had to get him out of her life, before he walked out of it on his own.

''Now here's the thing, Colin,'' she said, pacing again, pushing a hand through her hair, making it more than just a little spiky. ''Women fall all over you, right? Except I didn't. I'm the only one who didn't—and don't tell me that's not true, because you'd just be lying. What woman in her right mind wouldn't fall all over you?''

Colin held up his hand, one finger raised as he attempted to interrupt her. "Just for clarification here, and my own personal edification—does this mean you're not in your right mind?"

Holly frowned, mentally reviewed her last statement. "Scratch that. *Most* women in their right minds would fall all over you. I was—am, I mean *am*—the exception. And, man, did that ever rattle your cage, didn't it, Colin?"

"Rattling, rocking and rolling," he agreed, taking another step toward her so that, this time, it was her turn to hold out her hand, raise a finger to get his attention.

"But here's what you don't know," she told him quickly. "I figured it out. Not at first, definitely, but I figured it out, and decided on a small experiment tonight. If I wanted you to chase after me, all I had to do was keep telling you to go away. Be nasty, even rude. And you'd eat it up, keep coming back for more. And, damn, Colin, here you are. You're still here."

"Because I have a crush on you. Are you sure that's it? Maybe I'm a masochist?"

Holly rolled her eyes. "Don't be ridiculous. You're just being normal. Everyone wants what they can't have. You just never *couldn't have* before you met me. Admit it, Colin. Was there ever a woman you couldn't have?"

He mumbled something under his breath.

"What? What was that?" Holly asked, lifting a hand to her ear. "I couldn't hear you."

"I said, Miss Bartenski. My fourth-grade teacher. I had a crush on her."

"Aha!" Holly said, pleased. "Now we're getting somewhere. You *do* know what a crush is."

"Yes, Holly, I do. What I don't know is why you deliberately set out to be uncooperative, knowing that I'd become even more intrigued each time you treated me like gum on the bottom of your shoe that you were trying to scrape off. Why would you keep trying to attract me tonight, if you really wanted me to go away?"

Holly opened her mouth. Closed it. Shifted her gaze from side to side. "Oh," she said at last. "Um...it was an experiment? An...an intellectual exercise?"

He closed the space between them, put his hands on her shoulders. "I don't think so, Holly. Do you want to know what I think?"

"Probably not," she admitted, still trying to sort through her reactions, knowing darn full well that the *last* thing she really wanted was for Colin to go away.

"Too bad, because you're going to get it anyway. You have a crush on me, Holly Hollis. Shall we go over what constitutes a crush? Let's see, what was that? Oh, yes, I remember. It was something about wanting to kiss me until your toes curl up and you sigh into my mouth and melt against me, whisper my name over and over as I make love to you until we're both limp and spent and fall asleep in each other's arms—just so we can wake up and do it all again."

Holly resisted the urge to curl her bare toes into the carpet once more. "That was your explanation, not mine."

"True, but I like mine better. Don't you?"

Holly looked up at him. At that wonderful face, into those kind yet sexy eyes. "This is nuts."

"Probably," he agreed. "But as trying to get you to

admit to love at first sight doesn't appear to be an option, I think it's time we go with this crush idea of yours.''

"Meaning?''

"Meaning,'' he said, bending down and kissing her cheek, "I think we should spend the next week stuck together like glue, just to see what happens. If you're right, and we're both suffering from this crush syndrome, we'll get sick of each other by the time I have to go back to Paris. But,'' he added, his smile threatening to bring tears to her eyes, "if you're wrong, and I'm right, by the end of next week both our lives will have changed forever. So, is it a deal?''

"I don't know,'' Holly answered honestly.

"Well, that's honest. So I'll be honest, too. I don't want to let you go, Holly. And I won't let you go, go away, not without a fight.''

"You sure are Max's cousin, aren't you,'' Holly said, shaking her head. "Now I know what Julia was up against. Still, I also know I'm right on this one, Colin Rafferty, and if it takes having you around for the next week to prove it, then that's how it works.''

She bent her knees, effectively slipping out from under Colin's hands, and started for the hallway. "I'll get pillows and sheets for the couch. The larger one's a sleeper, as I'm pretty sure you already know. You can make yourself useful by tossing the cushions onto the other couch and opening it.''

"No rice bed, huh?'' Colin asked as she reentered the living room and threw a pillow and a set of sheets at his head.

"Not even in your dreams,'' she told him, then

turned on her heels, barely resisting the urge to *run* for the safety of her bedroom.

"Oh, definitely in my dreams, Holly," he called after her.

Holly slammed her bedroom door on a few choice, unlovely words she didn't want him to hear.

Chapter Seven

Colin woke to the aroma of frying bacon shortly after dawn the next morning, a grin on his face, his hopes high—and his lower back in a spasm, something he realized as he tried to sit up on the pull-out bed.

"Damn!" he swore, grabbing at his protesting back muscles as he staggered to his feet.

"Oh, that's lovely," Holly said, standing in the dining room, looking in at him. "Hair mussed, morning beard, and now he's bent over like an old man, scratching and moaning. Clearly this total immersion in each other isn't working to cool my mad, impulsive crush. Be still my heart."

He swiveled around, the muscle spasm easing slightly, and glared at her.

There she was, all spit and polish. Hair its usual intriguing spiky style, makeup on, dressed in stylishly baggy charcoal summer flannel slacks, crisp white silk blouse, and a black-and-burgundy paisley vest that hugged her slim waist, snugged against her rounded breasts. She wore softest gray leather, high-heeled boots that couldn't make her look much taller, but gave a whole new definition to the words "if you think I'm sexy."

"Oh, great, a morning person," he grumbled, heading toward the pair of travel bags he'd brought in from the BMW last night. "Where did you buy that sofa bed—Sadists Are Us? I think my back's broken in three places."

"Oh, you're just charming, Mr. Rafferty. Utterly charming. Breakfast in ten minutes. I put fresh towels in the bathroom for you. There's only one bathroom, so you're going to have to work around a few things I washed out this morning. Just deal with it, okay?"

"Why are we up so early? Should I quick shower and dress? Where are we going?"

"*I'm* going to work, I have no idea where *you're* going, although, if pushed, I certainly could make a few suggestions," Holly told him, then turned, a large, fairly lethal-looking fork held in front of her, and headed back to the kitchen.

"Not your smoothest this morning, are you, Rafferty?" Colin grumbled under his breath as he gathered up clean clothing, his shaving kit, and headed down the hallway, through Holly's bedroom, into the bathroom. He was greeted by the sight of three pair of still dripping panty hose draped over the glass door to the shower stall.

She'd done this on purpose, of course. He was pretty sure she would even have pulled three clean pair out of her dresser drawer and run them under the faucet, just so she could hang them up to bother him. She'd probably left the top off the toothpaste, too, and little blue globs of toothpaste in the bowl of the sink—just to turn him off.

Nope. No globs of toothpaste. She probably couldn't bring herself to be that messy. But she had "decorated" the counter around the sink with vials of lipstick, bottles of makeup, a bunch of brushes and pencils—and a small metal contraption he knew to be an eyelash curler, but had always thought of as the ladies' version of a cigar snipper.

How did she know he was a neat freak? Not *entirely* a neat freak, but his idea of a great way to start the morning had little to do with finding a spot for three pair of dripping-wet panty hose.

One by one, he gingerly lifted the sopping panty hose from the door, watched them plop down onto the floor, where they could dry, or twist themselves into knots. He really didn't care. Stripping out of the institutional gray cotton knit shorts and T-shirt he'd grabbed from his luggage last night, he stepped into the shower.

Nine minutes and twenty seconds later, still barefoot and unshaven, clad in faded jeans and a black T-shirt, he walked into the dining room, pulled out a chair and sat down. "Smells really good," he said, taking in the scrambled eggs, hash brown potatoes and two strips of bacon already sitting on his plate. "Looks good, too. Do you always decide what somebody else is going to eat?"

She hesitated as she spooned eggs onto her plate. "What do you mean?"

"I mean, you've loaded my plate for me, which

pretty much tells me you expect me to eat portions you've decided on. Now I'm looking at this stuff—and it really does smell good, honest—and trying to decide if you're trying to fatten me up, choke my arteries me with cholesterol, or make sure I don't eat *three* pieces of bacon.''

Holly sat back in her chair, blinked. "I...I never *thought* of that. Mom just always loaded up our plates for us in the kitchen, to save on serving dishes, all those extra dishes to wash. But you're right, Colin. Mom was, in a way, deciding how much or how little us kids would eat. Why would she do such a thing? How...how *controlling*. Dad, too, like she was in charge of all our appetites. And now I'm doing the same thing. I'm so sorry!''

"So am I," Colin said, digging in to his scrambled eggs. "I didn't mean to give you something to tell a shrink. Your mom was probably just trying to save on dirty plates, just like you said. Makes sense to me. However, that said, I hope you won't mind if I butter my own toast.''

Holly blinked, looked at the knife she held in her right hand, the piece of toast clutched in her left. "This...this is for me.''

"Sure, and the two already buttered pieces on your plate are for me, right?''

He considered it a small blessing that she threw the toast at him, and not the butter knife.

Holly plopped her elbows on the table and dropped her head into her hands. "Oh God, I'm my mother! This can't be!'' Then she sat back once more, glared at him. "Well, thanks, Colin, thanks a whole heap. I could have gone through my entire life without realizing I'm turning into my own mother. Next thing you know I'll be telling you to sit up at the table, don't slouch, because it will ruin your digestion. I think I'm going to be sick!''

Colin chuckled under his breath. He just adored it when she took off, flew straight into the sky with her dramatic responses. He didn't know why, he just did. ''I don't know what you're so upset about, Holly. I'll bet your mother is a wonderful woman. Caring, protective…''

''Smothering,'' Holly added, making a face. ''Just wait until you meet her.''

''I'm going to meet her? When?''

Holly didn't answer. She looked at the slim watch on her wrist, then dug into her breakfast, once more eating with an obvious appreciation for the food that went into her mouth, and not picking like an anorexic bird— meaning most every woman he'd ever shared a meal with over the years.

''Holly? I am going to meet her, right? Wasn't there something about Sunday dinners at your parents' house? It's Friday. I don't leave for Paris until next Friday, remember? In the meantime, we're doing this immersion-aversion therapy, which means I go where you go.''

''And to think that it all sounded so logical last night. I must have been out of my mind,'' Holly grumbled, standing up, lifting her plate.

''Leave it,'' Colin offered, waving toward the plate. ''I know you said you have to get in to the office early this morning. I'll clean up, which is only fair, because you cooked, and I'll meet you at the offices around noon, so we can go to lunch together. I hope you don't mind if I use your phone to make a few calls to my Paris office. I'll use my company credit card, I promise.''

Holly looked at him, looked toward the kitchen—he could see the stove from his chair, and three frying pans sat on it. Looked at him again. "Okay," she said, nodding her head in agreement. "I cooked, the least you can do is clean up. And close up the sofa bed, please." Then she smiled. "I like this," she said, waggling her eyebrows evilly. "I've never bossed anyone around before."

"Now why do I doubt that?" Colin said, heading for the hall closet, taking out a thin pale gray trench coat and helping her into it. "Just in case you haven't noticed that it's drizzling out there," he said, turning down her collar, then pulling her toward him, planting a kiss on her soft, pink lips. He released her slowly, smiling as he looked down at her, at her still-closed eyes, her slightly open mouth.

"I like this," he said, waggling his eyebrows much as she had just done. "I've never worried about anyone before."

Holly closed the door of her 4x4 and sat back against the seat, trying to catch her breath.

Oh God, he was gorgeous.

He'd been gorgeous before, but with his hair sort of mussed, his eyes still sleepy, that shadow of beard on his cheeks? Definitely more than gorgeous.

Did he have to wear shorts? She'd always heard, and agreed, that a man's butt was a wonderful thing, but it had never occurred to her that she could go slightly gaga over a pair of wonderfully straight legs covered in soft black hair.

She knew the hair was soft—as soft as his calves were hard—because she'd actually touched him the other day, to goad him into lifting up his leg so she could help him take off his shoes.

And his shoulders? She let out her breath in a rush, remembering how he'd looked in his black T-shirt just now. What straight shoulders, what a wonderfully flat belly. The guy had been sculpted by a master.

She'd seen him in an Armani suit. She'd seen him in a tux. But she'd melted completely this morning, seeing him as just Colin Rafferty, very, *very* healthy male animal.

Physical attraction. That's what it was, nothing less, nothing more. A very immediate and extremely *intense* physical attraction. There couldn't be any other explanation for her immediate and complete *awareness* of this man.

Holly inserted the key into the ignition and backed out of her parking space before she could give in to impulse and return to her apartment, jump the man's bones.

"And wouldn't that be *adult* of me," Holly grumbled as she drove through the maze of smaller streets that led to the entrance ramp to Route 22 and her trip to the office. "You didn't jump into bed with Richard, and he was gorgeous."

She tapped her fingers on the steering wheel as she tried to conjure up a vision of Richard's face. Handsome yes, but sort of *fleshy,* now that she really thought about it. And his smile never quite got as far as his eyes—to avoid ugly crow's-feet, of course.

And he always had a manicure. That had always bothered her. She couldn't seem to get past the idea of Richard sitting in some beauty salon, his fingertips stuck in a bowl of soapy water, letting clear polish be painted onto his fingernails. Did he wear a smock, maybe one with flowers on it, like they had at her beauty salon? Did he have pedicures, too? *Eeeuuuwww!*

Not that her heart would go pitty-pat for a guy with ragged, unkempt nails, grease blackening his fingertips, but there had to be a happy medium, didn't there?

Colin's hands were a marvel. His palms were nearly square, his fingers long, with clean, blunt-cut nails—and no polish. She'd been fascinated watching his hands last night, as he'd played her grandfather's guitar. Talented hands. Talented fingers.

How would they feel if he "played" those hands and fingers over her?

A horn honking behind her alerted Holly to the fact that she was on MacArthur Road now, somehow having exited Route 22 without realizing it, and that the streetlight in front of her had turned green.

"You've got to stop this," she told herself as she continued on to the office connected to the new Sutherland offices, a large, modern factory situated on Front Street. "You've got to get this guy out of your system, one way or another."

She parked the Jeep, then just sat there, staring out the windshield. What was she worrying about? Next Friday he was going back to Paris. It would be kind of difficult to maintain a crush on a guy three thousand miles away.

"So you'd better get him out of your system now, because otherwise you'll be all alone, listening to tear-jerker golden oldies on the radio every Saturday night and crying into your brownie batter," she warned herself.

Of course, she realized as she opened her car door and grabbed her leather briefcase, that meant that Colin's "immersion-aversion" plan, as he called it, just might be a good one.

She could really hate him for that.

"Crush, smush—the whole idea is crazy and I'm crazy for considering it, let alone bringing it up in the first place, then going along with his solution. Some solution! I should have just kept my big mouth shut, sent him away and eaten a half gallon of Rocky Road to get him out of my system."

"Hi, Holly, talking to yourself again? You really might want to consider carrying one of those portable tape recorders around with you, just so nobody sees you, locks you up in a rubber room."

Holly turned to see Jim Sutherland approaching, looking fit and healthy, and remarkably handsome for a man in his early sixties. Both Jim and Margaret Sutherland were good-looking people—which did a lot to explain her friend Julia's classic good looks.

"Morning, Jim. You're here early," she said, ignoring his teasing as she fell into step beside him, heading for the door to the office.

"We're wrapping up the Corrigin order today. You and Julia should be very proud of yourselves. They took the whole line, for twenty-five of their top-line department stores. That's quite a coup.''

"Yeah," Holly said, inserting her key into the lock, then pushing open the door to the private offices, motioning for Jim to precede her as she went straight to the alarm system and punched in the proper code. "Julia's wanted to get into the Southwest for a couple of years now, and she's finally done it. Where's Wellington?''

Jim looked down at his side, as if he expected the huge, loving black dog to be there, which he wasn't. "Oh, yeah, I forgot. Margaret's taking him to the vet today, for his regular checkup, and won't drop him off until after lunch. Let's hope the bad guys stay away, with our official watchdog taking the morning off.''

Holly laughed as she shrugged out of her raincoat and hung it on the antique clothes tree. "Wellington? A watchdog? What would he do to the bad guys, Jim. Give them the combination to the safe?''

Jim laughed, gave Holly a wave and passed through the doorway that led to the huge factory, where over a hundred sewing machines were already buzzing.

Turning on lights, starting the coffeemaker, Holly gave a few moments thought to Wellington. Technically he was still Julia's dog, but neither she nor Max had the heart to coop the animal up in a New York condo, so they'd left him with Jim and Margaret. Jim brought Wellington to work with him every day, and the two went for walks at lunchtime, making Jim's cardiac exercise more enjoyable. The plan worked beautifully, for everyone.

Holly remembered Julia telling her how Max had

come back into her life and Wellington—traitor that he was—had immediately made a fool out of himself, almost wagging his tail clean off to impress Max.

Dogs and kids. Theirs was a judgment a person could trust. Wellington had known at once that Max was one of the good guys, even though it had riled Julia at the time. How would Wellington react to Colin? He'd be here at lunchtime. Wellington would be here at lunchtime.

Was she up for a small experiment? Would Jim mind if she borrowed Wellington today? "Oh, Jim," Holly called out, heading into the factory before she could change her mind.

Colin realized he was whistling as he scrubbed out the frying pan coated in bacon grease. Whistling? He didn't whistle. He didn't hum, either, or at least he hadn't done that in a lot of years. Not since he'd left the band, packed away his guitar, started playing grown-up at Majestic Enterprises.

He really had to get a grip here. Whistling? For pity's sake—whistling?

There was a small radio on the end of the counter, and he turned it on, found it already dialed-in to an oldies' station. He cranked up the volume.

He slid the frying pan into the dishwasher, reached for another pan and found himself singing along with the first few bars of "Old Time Rock and Roll."

He rinsed the pan, fitted it into the dishwasher, flipped the door shut and grabbed the dishcloth that lay on the countertop.

He began pounding out the beat with the heel of his

right foot as he wiped the counters, his voice growing stronger as he sang about loving that old-time rock and roll. He danced his way into the dining room, twirling the dishcloth over his head, then wiped the tabletop as he kept up the beat, let himself *go* with the music.

Toeing off his sneakers, he eyed the shiny surface of the kitchen floor, then launched himself onto it, sliding all the way to the sink as he did his best Tom Cruise imitation, still singing at the top of his lungs, doing a little gyrating to the beat just like good old Tom had done in that movie years earlier. What movie was that? Oh, yeah, *Risky Business*. Okay, that fit. He was into some pretty risky business himself at the moment.

His shoulders moved, his hips shook, he picked up a serving spoon and held it to his mouth like a microphone, then turned to do another slide, back to the dining room.

And then he stopped. Stopped dead in midhip-thrust. Wanted to drop dead.

"*Who* are you?" a rather petite, aging-well woman holding a brown paper bag filled with groceries said. She was eyeing him balefully, her wide green eyes raking him from white socks to uncombed hair, then back again.

"Um…hello," Colin said, then realized he still held the spoon like a microphone. He dropped his arm, tossed the spoon behind him, in the general direction of the sink. "That is," he said, dragging out his best "trust me, I'm harmless" smile, "good morning, Mrs. Hollis. You *are* Mrs. Hollis, aren't you? Holly looks just like you."

Hillary Hollis tipped her head to one side, raised her

eyebrows. "You know Holly," she said as she brushed past him, deposited the grocery bag on the counter. "That's good. Although I didn't really think you broke in here, slept on that terrible pull-out couch, then made yourself breakfast. Do you have a name?"

"I used to," Colin answered, grinning, "except I'm having trouble remembering it just now." He held out his right hand. "Ah, it's all coming back to me now. It's Colin. Colin Rafferty."

Hillary shook his hand, then went back to unloading groceries. "Rafferty? As in Max Rafferty?" she asked, handing him a loaf of bread and pointing to the wicker basket on the end of the counter. "Thank God. I thought she'd broken her vow never to date another male model. Handsome devil, aren't you? You're not a male model?"

"No, ma'am," Colin promised her. "I work with Max, in Paris. I...Holly and I met through Max and Julia, and I followed her here from New York because I'm crazy about her."

"Or just plain crazy," Hillary offered sweetly, switching off the radio just as the song ended. "I saw that movie. Saw it twice, actually, and I've always wondered if I would have the guts to do what you were doing. Was it fun?"

"A lot of fun, yes," Colin told her, leaning back against the kitchen counter. "I did sleep on that couch, Mrs. Hollis. Honest."

"I'm sure you did. I trust my daughter, Mr. Rafferty. Oh, not to have proper food in the house, but I do trust her to behave herself."

Behave herself? That was a mother's expression if

ever Colin had heard one. He coughed into his fist, then said, "Would you like a cup of coffee, Mrs. Hollis? There's still some left in the pot."

Hillary put the half gallon of milk in the refrigerator, closed the door. "I'd love some, thank you, but not if Holly made it. Why don't you go clean up in the living room, put on your sneakers and I'll make up a fresh pot. One that won't quite grow hair on your chest."

"Yes, ma'am," Colin said, picking up his sneakers, and hiding his rather warm cheeks. His movements were clumsy, and he somehow turned the bow on his right sneaker into a knot as he tried to untie it. He hadn't felt this out of step since his elementary school days.

"Oh, and please call me Hillary. One more *yes, ma'am* and I'll think I'm in my dotage."

"Yes mm—yes, *Hillary*. Thank you."

He escaped to the living room, gathering up the sheets and piling them in the center of the mattress before shoving the whole works back into the base of the couch. He replaced the cushions, the pillows, and carried his own pillow into the bedroom, tossed it on Holly's bed.

Running a hand over his lower jaw, he decided he'd gone native long enough, rescued his portable electric razor from his shaving kit and got rid of his morning beard. He looked at his reflection in the mirror over the bathroom sink, and then he grinned.

"You're *scared* of her," he told himself. "She's Holly's mother, she holds a lot of influence over her daughter, and you're scared spitless that you just made the mother of bad first impressions. God, Rafferty, this must be love."

"Colin!" Hillary called from the kitchen. "Coffee's ready if you are."

He joined Hillary in the dining room, pushing back a smile as he looked at the already poured cup of coffee at his place setting, and the small dessert plate with three cookies on it. He wondered what would happen if he asked for four.

Hillary saw him eyeing the cookies. "They're store-bought, but really very good. I just don't seem to have time to bake anymore. Did Holly tell you that I baby-sit Herb and Nancy's three during the week? Well, I only have Mark all day...the twins are in second grade now, although summer vacations can really wear me out. So, why did you sleep on my daughter's couch? Are you hoping for better luck tonight?"

Colin spit coffee into his napkin as he coughed and choked. Hillary was behind him immediately, slapping him on the back, telling him to put his arms up over his head, because that had always worked with her children when "something went down the wrong pipe."

Colin wiped at his chin, blinked his stinging eyes. "Mrs. Hollis—Hillary—I really think I need to explain something to you."

"No, you don't," she said breezily as she returned to her chair. "Although I have a small confession for you. I already knew your name. Julia phoned me last night. Then Max got on the line. By the time they were finished, I pretty much knew everything there is to know. Why else do you think I'm here so early this morning, if not to catch a glimpse of the man who thinks he's going to marry my baby? I hope you didn't mind that crack about the male models? Max said I had to say that. But it was Julia's idea that I stop by this morning, once I was sure Holly's Jeep was gone, and surprise you.''

By now, Colin had regained his slightly shattered composure. ''Boy, when Max says Julia gets more than even, he wasn't just kidding. Did she, that is, did they tell you what happened the other day?''

''About Holly mistaking you for a male model? Oh, yes, I heard it all. And I saw you, just this morning, on an advertisement for the fashion special on CNN next week. You and a model, coming down the runway, then you kissing her. Have you seen it yet?''

''They're using the bit I was in for the *promo?* Oh, boy. Please tell me this isn't going out internationally. Everyone I know in Paris watches CNN.''

''I really wouldn't know,'' Hillary said, picking up her plate and mug and heading for the kitchen. He followed her.

''Holly wants me to leave town, you know. Probably wants me to leave the country.''

''That sounds like Holly. But Julia assured me that you're sincere, that you really do care for her and that she was immediately struck with you. Howard, that's Holly's father, and I met one week, became engaged the next. We haven't been sorry yet, and we'll be married thirty-eight years in February. So you see, I'm a firm believer in the validity of love at first sight. I'd have to be, wouldn't I?''

She loaded the plates and mugs into the dishwasher, added liquid detergent, turned it on, then looked up at the clock hanging on the wall. ''Oh, would you look at the time!'' she exclaimed, picking up her purse and heading for the door—demonstrating to Colin just where Holly had inherited her fleetness of foot.

"You're leaving?"

"I'm afraid so. I only grabbed a few things at the corner store to come over here and spy on you, so now I have to brave the Saturday crush at the supermarket for the rest of the things I need for Sunday dinner. Do you like rump roast? I make a fabulous rump roast."

Colin leaned down and kissed Hillary's cheek. "I love rump roast, thank you. Thank you for everything."

"Don't thank me," Hillary said, giving herself a small shake. "Holly keeps swearing she'll never marry, that she doesn't want children. Of course, she only says that for self-protection, poor thing, because she's been unlucky a few times. If Julia and Max are right, if Holly has fallen hard for you—and you're half the man they both say you are—I should be thanking you. I've been waiting for this for years. *Years!*"

And then she was gone, having blown in and out of the apartment like a minihurricane, and Colin was left to sit on the couch, shake his head and then lay back, laughing until tears rolled down his cheeks.

Then he sobered, reached for the television remote control and started channel-surfing until he located CNN. How in hell was he going to explain this to some of the more straitlaced executives he dealt with in Paris? And did he care?

No, he decided after only a few moments. He didn't care. How could he, when that walk down the runway had led him straight to the woman he was determined to make his wife?

* * *

Well, there went another experiment, straight to hell.

Holly made a face behind Colin's back as he leaned forward on the park bench and rubbed Wellington's belly.

Rotten dog. He'd taken one look at Colin, sniffed at his shoes for a moment and then turned into a tongue-lolling, tail-wagging sycophant.

"So this is the great Wellington?" Collin had said, scratching the delighted dog behind the ears. "To hear Max tell it, the main reason he and Julia are building a home here in Allentown is so that they can see more of Wellington. I don't blame them. He's a real sweet-heart."

"Yeah, I get all choked up every time I see him myself," Holly had told him sourly as she'd pulled on the dog's leash, heading out of the office.

Now, forty-five minutes later, the remnants of their fast-food lunch were stuffed into the paper bag and tossed in a wire waste can in the park. Holly had downed two hamburgers, Colin the same, and Wellington had pigged out on three, plus half of Holly's French fries.

"He needs exercise," Holly told Colin, and reached in her huge purse, pulling out a large rawhide bone. "Jim says to throw it and Wellington will play fetch until it's time to go back to work."

"Sounds like a plan," Colin said, taking the bone from her, showing it to Wellington and then tossing it out over the grass. The dog was off like a shot, his black coat gleaming in the sun as he covered ground with remarkable speed.

"So," Colin said as Wellington, the bone now in his mouth, was sidetracked by three small children who wanted to pet him. He laid down, raised all four paws in the air and let them scratch his belly. "Now that Wellington's taken care of, how was your morning? Busy?"

Holly nodded. "The whole place is a madhouse. We've got the workers all on Saturday overtime because we have to finish a huge order today. Faxes are piling up, which is a good thing, because most of them are orders for the new bridal wear. Our only blessing is that nobody's phoning us, as everyone must think we're closed for the weekend. Otherwise, I wouldn't even have been able to steal away for lunch."

"You love it, don't you? The rush, the hassles, the pressure?"

Holly was about to agree, but then she stopped herself. Thought about it for a moment. "I don't know," she said at last. "I mean, I *do* love my job. I like feeling like a success. I *am* a success, darn it."

"But you're not sure if this is what you want to do for the rest of your life?"

Holly looked at him, feeling uncomfortable, and not knowing why. A week ago she'd been happy. Not delirious, not in her personal life anyway, but her job had never been anything but a joy. In fact, she'd pretty much talked herself into the idea that she'd been born to be a career woman. A good aunt, yes, but with no kids of her own. A good daughter, but never a mother. Never a wife.

Oh, maybe someday. Someday she'd meet somebody, somebody with mutual interests—maybe they'd share a liking for the same arthritis medicine, the same flavor of powdered fiber. Just two over-the-hill types who'd decided that together was better than alone.

And wasn't *that* depressing!

When she didn't answer, Colin pushed at her. "I've been told that you've pretty much decided never to marry, never to have kids."

She swung around on the bench, glared at him. "Who told you that?"

He grinned, and Holly felt her stomach go into a knot. "Your mother?" he half offered, half questioned, and then quickly raised his hands in front of his face—which was a good thing, because Holly immediately longed to grab his throat and wring the rest of the story out of him.

"My *mother?*" She jumped up from the bench, pressed one hand against her spine, the other to her forehead—the drama queen going into action, although she didn't notice; she was too angry. "My mother. Of course. Why not? Julia. Max. And now my mother. And did you tell her about this stupid crush thing? Our immersion-aversion experiment? Oh, of course you did. You couldn't resist, and Mom just gobbled it all up, didn't she? That's it! Experiment's over! I'm outta here!"

And the rat, the dirty rat, just sat there and let her go. Probably because he knew, as she knew, that she really had nowhere to run....

Chapter Eight

They ate dinner at a local restaurant that night, one of those small, homey places where the menu selections were almost limitless and everybody knew everybody else.

Colin and Holly were stopped no less than five times on the way to their table, and each time Holly had to introduce him to friends of her parents, friends of her siblings, former high school classmates.

It was like old home week, except that Holly, although polite, didn't seem to be overjoyed to introduce him—especially to Melissa Harbrook, who kept eyeing him like he was a juicy slice of prime rib, and she liked her men rare. Hey, he wasn't blind. He noticed this stuff.

"There was a place a lot like this near my off-campus rooms at Princeton," Colin said once they were seated, looking around the No-Smoking section of the restaurant, at the owner's collection of ceramic cows lining shelves high on all four walls. "Not the cows, though. That's pretty original."

"I never liked Melissa Harbrook," Holly said, opening the menu. "Or should I say Melissa Johnson Whittier Harbrook. The woman goes through men like a hot knife through butter." Her gaze left the mimeographed page of Specials and she glared at him. "You want her number? I'm surprised she just doesn't have it tattooed on her forehead, right next to that flashing Open All Night sign."

"Yes, she was sort of giving me the eye, wasn't she?" Colin asked, helpfully adding fuel to the fire of Holly's temper. She hadn't returned to the apartment until nearly five and, as far as he could remember, this was only the second time she'd spoken to him since then. The first time had been when she'd stood just inside the front door, her car keys in her hand, and grumbled, "You hungry or what? I'm going to dinner."

That was his Holly, gracious to the max.

"How long do they go on?" he asked her after a moment. "Your bad moods, that is."

"Bad moods?" Holly looked around at the other tables, then lowered her voice, repeated herself. "Bad moods? You think this is a bad mood? You don't think I have just the tiniest bit of *justification* here? I've got a conspiracy working against me. You, Julia, Max, my own *mother,* for crying out loud. And maybe you don't know about the telephone call I got at work this afternoon. Oh, yes. Helen called. Big sister, out to give advice, so that little sis doesn't screw this one up because Mom says Colin Rafferty is a real keeper. Bad mood? You're all lucky I'm not homicidal! And does anyone stop to think that maybe you're *stalking* me? Huh? No, they don't. They think this is cute. Well, let me tell you something, Colin Rafferty, *I* don't think this is cute anymore."

"Stalking you?" Colin closed his menu, looked at her closely. "Is that what you really think, Holly? That I'm *stalking* you?"

She avoided his eyes. "No, I don't think you're stalking me. I ran away, you followed, and I let you sleep on my sofa bed. If you're stalking, I'm aiding and abetting. I just...I just think we're going too fast here. I'm...I'm scared, much as I hate to admit it."

"It's that crush thing," Colin said, nodding his head. "That sort of instant *knowing* that there was something special between us. But while I'm enjoying the hell out of it, the whole idea is scaring you silly. I understand. I'll go back to New York tomorrow, give you some space, some time. Some room."

"No!"

Now heads did turn, and Holly's cheeks flushed bright red as she lowered her head, motioned for him to lean closer across the table. "I don't want you to go back to New York," she said, nearly whispered.

He was so tempted to lean forward, cup a hand behind one ear and ask her to repeat that, because he hadn't heard it. But he decided not to push his luck. "Good," he said instead, unfolding his paper napkin and putting it on his lap. "Because your mom's making rump roast tomorrow, for dinner. So maybe you'll want chicken tonight, instead of beef?"

Holly pressed her palms to her cheeks. "Sunday dinner. Oh my God, I completely forgot. All the *H*'s, all their kiddies, Grandma Hollis. And the neighbor ladies who will just stop in, unexpectedly, to borrow a cup of sugar, drop off tickets to some show at the local playhouse, be introduced to Holly's *beau*. I can't stand it.''

Colin bit his lip to keep from laughing out loud. ''I think your mother is a lovely woman.''

Holly nodded. ''Oh, she's great, really.''

''And your family? They're all great, too?''

''Great family,'' Holly agreed, playing with the milk-glass vase on the table, the one with the pink silk flowers in it, some of the petals rather singed because they drooped over the blue glass jars with a burning candle inside, and had ''wilted'' from the heat. ''Really great family.''

''I spoke to Julia this afternoon when she called to check up on us. She suggested you take next week off, don't go to the office.''

Holly kept her head down, but raised her eyes to look at him. Dear Lord but those green eyes of hers were potent; full of every emotion she felt, and some she refused to acknowledge. A man could spend a lifetime, quite happily, just watching her face, that wonderful little pixie face.

''Julia...Julia said that? But we're swamped at work. Irene will be back in the office on Monday, but—''

''Julia's coming into town tomorrow, to visit her folks, and to spend a week at the office. She says she thinks she can handle your job while you're gone.''

And there went the eyes! Narrowed, intense. ''You're ganging up on me, aren't you? All of you.''

Colin didn't answer, as the waitress appeared to take their orders. Holly selected grilled boneless chicken and fried filling, with a side of cold pickled cabbage. "Same for me, thank you," he told the waitress, then handed her his menu.

Once the woman had moved away, he leaned forward and asked, "What the hell is fried filling?"

Holly grinned, momentarily sidetracked. "Well, you won't get it in Paris, that's for sure," she told him. "It's potato filling—mashed potatoes, bread cubes, celery, onions, some raw egg mixed in, I think, all baked in the oven. You know, filling, stuffing, whatever you want to call it. Except that the night of Helen's rehearsal dinner for her wedding, we were all held up at the church, and the owner—that would be Bob—had to put all the filling on the grill because it was drying out too much in the oven. Good idea, except we were really, *really* late, and by the time we got here—fried filling. All soft and wonderful on the inside, crisp and brown on the outside. I've been ordering it that way ever since, and Bob makes it up special for me. More than you needed to know, huh?"

Colin rubbed his hands together. "Not really. So I'm having, essentially, fried mashed potatoes?"

"Essentially, yes. And you'll love it, I promise. So don't be picky, okay? Bob gets upset when people don't like his food."

Colin grinned. "Can I put ketchup on it?"

Holly rolled her eyes, then grinned back at him. Did he know how to make her smile, or what? And how he loved to make her smile. "*No-o-o,* you can't put catsup on it. I'll bet you ate snails in Paris."

"I'll bet I didn't," he told her, making a face. "I told

you, I really missed American food. Fried filling possibly being the exception.''

Mention of Paris seemed to take Holly off in yet another direction. ''Is Paris the only Majestic Enterprises office you've ever worked in for Max?''

''No. I cut my teeth in his Pittsburgh office, then moved to New York for a while. But, since I was relatively young, and definitely unattached, Paris seemed a good option when the opening came up.''

She played with her fork, turning it over and over on the tabletop. ''And you can't wait to get back there?''

Now she was fishing, and he loved it. ''I *have* to get back there. Unfinished business, and all of that. I told you, I won't be back in the States until Christmas. After that? Who knows. Majestic Enterprises is just about everywhere, so I'll probably pretty much have my pick of exotic locations. England. Brussels.'' He hesitated, then ended, ''New Jersey.''

''New—'' Holly sort of coughed, reached for her water glass, while Colin waited, smiling. ''New Jersey, huh? I'd forgotten that Julia told me Max had just bought a property there. Some huge office complex?''

''Two-year-old building, and the company that built it just merged with another telecommunications giant, so that their headquarters have moved south, to Atlanta, I think. Max thought it was the perfect opportunity to consolidate our own main offices, all in one place. Forty-five minutes from New York, only about an hour from Allentown. It's another reason he and Julia are going to build a home here. Julia can be nearer her own business and her parents, Jim and Margaret can see plenty of Max Deuce, and everybody's happy.''

"I really have to pay more attention," Holly grumbled almost under her breath. "I've been so caught up with this new bridal wear line that half of anything somebody tells me goes—*pffftt!*—straight over my head."

"But you did hear that I want to marry you? I'd really be depressed to think that one went—*pffftt!*—straight over your head."

And there went the eyes—going from a soft confused green, straight to emerald ice.

"Will you *please* cut that out," Holly asked him, just about begged him. "You've got Julia going, you've got Max going—and my mother is probably already tying up sugared almonds in little net bags, for favors for the guests at the wedding. My only consolation at this point is that all of the Hollis family is going to descend on you like a ton of bricks tomorrow. And I won't even feel sorry for you."

"If we're here," Colin said as the waitress placed plates in front of them, then added small bowls of pickled cabbage, a basket of bread, and told them to enjoy their dinner. She didn't ask them to enjoy their dinner; she told them. "Enjoy your dinner." He liked that. He'd really missed places like this homey restaurant.

He picked up his fork, tentatively poked at the brown thing sitting beside the chicken breast. "Smells good," he said, then took a bite, smiled. Homey-gourmet, a whole new dining experience.

Then he looked at Holly, who still hadn't picked up knife or fork. "What?" he asked, motioning toward her plate. "Aren't you hungry?"

She ignored his question for one of her own. "What

did you mean, *if we're here?* Where else would we be?"

"Interesting question, Holly. Where else could we be? I don't go back to Paris until the end of next week. You have the week off, if you take Julia up on her offer. It's September, still warm, but the schools are open, so Ocean City should be fairly quiet. The beach, the boardwalk, maybe a trip north to visit a casino? Time to talk, time to get to know each other better, a clear field for carrying out our immersion-aversion plan?"

Holly sat back in her chair, blinking at him.

"But…but my mother…"

"Oh, yes. Rump roast. I forgot."

"And everyone else? My brothers, my sister? My dad playing twenty questions with you over how well you could take care of his baby?"

"Sounds wonderful," Colin said, his grin wicked. "Maybe you're right, Holly. Maybe we should stay here. And then, when Julia gets to town on Monday, well, I imagine we'll be invited to dinner at Margaret and Jim's house. Not that Julia would play twenty questions with me. She'd probably pretty much reserve that for you."

Holly still hadn't touched her dinner. "My family's really very nice."

"Your mother is a wonderful woman," Colin agreed, taking another bite of fried filling. "I'm sure the rest of your family is just as wonderful."

"And Julia," Holly persisted. "She's my very best friend in the whole world."

"Julia's also wonderful," Colin said, just trying to be cooperative.

"Of course, we wouldn't have much time alone together, not if you're going back to Paris next weekend."

"There is that," Colin put in, shoveling a forkful of pickled cabbage into his mouth, hoping its tartness would keep him from grinning. Holly was being very helpful.

"But, if we did this, it would be strictly platonic. Separate rooms."

"Absolutely," Colin said firmly. "I don't want you taking unfair advantage of me just because I think you can."

"*Me?* Take unfair advantage of *you?*" Holly shook her head. "I must be out of my mind to even be *discussing* this. It's silly, stupid. Impossible."

"So we'll leave tomorrow morning? Can you be ready by eight?" Colin asked.

"By eight," Holly agreed, then picked up her fork and dug in to her fried filling. "First to church, and then to sin city...I mean, Ocean City."

Holly was still in a state of shock.

"Hi, Mom," she'd said into the phone around seven Sunday morning, as she and her mother shared the habit of rising early, getting a good start on the day. "I heard you met Colin yesterday. Funny thing about that, Mom. We're really hitting it off, but he's got to go back to Paris next weekend, so we decided it might be fun to get away together this week. Ocean City, just for a few days."

"I see," her mother said, and Holly had known that, yes indeed, her mother "saw." Her mother *saw* everything, which was why none of the Hollis children had gotten away with much without being caught. "That sounds logical. We are a bit of a crowd, aren't we? And Helen—she's such a romantic—is already going all silly on me, talking about love at first sight, and showers and weddings and more grandchildren. I don't know where that girl gets it, do you?"

Holly had bitten her bottom lip, wondering what side of the bed her mother had gotten up on—the silly side? "We're going to have separate rooms, Mom. No hanky-panky, as Grandma would call it."

"Well, that's depressing," her mother had said… which was pretty much when Holly had lost track of the conversation. She knew she'd apologized for missing Sunday dinner and asked her mother to pass along her apology to her dad. She was pretty sure she'd promised to wear her seat belt, and even to remind Colin that her mom said I-95 could be a real speedway sometimes. But, other than that, the rest of the telephone call remained pretty much a blur.

Now here she was, sitting in the passenger seat—seat belt on—riding along the Atlantic City Expressway, agreeing with Colin that, yes, they should take Exit 7S and head into Ocean City via the Ninth Street Bridge.

"I still can't believe I said yes to this," she told him, probably for the tenth time in two hours. "I am *not* an impulsive person."

"No, of course you're not. You're calm, collected, steady as a rock. Never panic, never jump to conclusions, never take things too seriously, never overreact." He turned to her, grinned. "And I'm the King of Siam."

Holly slumped down in her seat, pushed her chin

against her chest. "I don't sound the least bit appealing."

"Oh, you're appealing, Holly. Damn appealing."

"Really," Holly said, not in the least flattered. "I think I'm bossy, headstrong, prone to exaggerate problems, and…and short."

"Petite. Isn't that what you guys in the fashion industry call it? Petite?"

"Short is short. Not that I have a complex about it or anything. Except for those times I'm surrounded by all those tall, gorgeous models. I keep telling Julia that the world is not made up of skinny tall people. Thankfully she agrees, and designs her clothing for all shapes and sizes, although she still uses all those top models in her shows. People expect it, I guess. And I spend the day feeling like a small town munchkin in a land of glamorous giants."

"You know, I didn't notice a single one of those models. All I saw was you. The tiny human dynamo, center of the tornado, the real life and sparkle standing out so clearly in the middle of that madness. You blew me away, Holly. No kidding. Even if you hadn't told me to drop my pants."

She looked over at him, stared at him as he fished in his pocket, passed bills over to the toll taker. "I'm still insisting on separate rooms," she told him, trying to convince herself.

Colin threw back his head and laughed as he pulled out of the tollbooth. "Oh, Holly, this is going to be a great couple of days."

Holly stood in front of the full-length mirror in the narrow hallway of her motel room, wondering if her

Rod Stewart-type spiky hairdo went well with a fairly romantic, ankle-length sundress.

"Maybe not a real great look for Rod, but you look pretty good," she assured herself, then headed into the bathroom behind her, to find her Perfectly Plum lipstick that matched the dominant color in the floral-design cotton dress.

They'd been in Ocean City for two days—it felt like two minutes. Or two lifetimes.

Sunday, they'd pretty much spent the day traveling, finding a suitable hotel, unpacking and eating a clam dinner that had left Holly stuffed, and sleepy, and ready for an early night. Surprisingly Colin had agreed, and gone off to his own room, on a completely different floor of the hotel, without more than a single kiss goodnight.

The fact that this kiss had lasted for a good two minutes probably meant something. It certainly had to Holly, who was still trying to figure out why Colin was attracted to her...and why she still asked herself why.

Was she really that unsure of her own attraction to men?

Was her experience with Richard, to name one, still keeping her wary of men—especially the Greek god type?

Was she afraid to fall as fast and hard as she knew she was falling?

What of her career, her life-plan, her firmly stated resolutions? One pretty face and they all went out the window? Was she that shallow?

Or was Colin Rafferty so wonderful, so *right,* that it was only the rest of her world that was wrong?

The lipstick slipped in her hand, sliding a Perfectly Plum streak onto her chin as Colin rapped three times on the motel room door. "You ready yet, Holly? Because I'm starving."

"I'm coming, I'm coming!" she called out, grabbing a handful of tissues and wiping at the smeared lipstick. She glanced at her watch, saw that he was five minutes early. They'd had a late breakfast after a walk on the beach, then spent the afternoon at the zoo in Cape May.

Colin had held her hand, playfully talked back to the monkeys, and bought her a bottle of insect repellent before he'd allow her to walk the paths that wandered through an area heavily populated with deer, just so she wouldn't be bitten by a deer tick, get Lyme disease and never forgive him for it.

"And because I'm getting a real kick out of rubbing this stuff on your back and neck," he'd told her, then turned her in his arms, kissed her long and hard, until a peacock strolling by screeched, probably in protest at seeing someone more beautiful than its feathered, manly self.

So now, showered and changed, they were off to the boardwalk for dinner. Holly grabbed her huge shoulder bag, hefted its weight, then tossed the thing onto the bed. She was on vacation, and didn't need her cell phone or her daily planner, or anything else.

"Ready to go," she said, opening the door, then handing him her key card, because there were no pockets in her sundress. "I'm not carrying my wallet, so dinner's your treat." Then she looked up at him, her eyes wide. "Glasses. You're wearing glasses? I didn't know you wore contact lenses."

"You didn't?" he asked, putting his arm around her as they walked to the elevator. "I guess we haven't gotten that far in our immersion-aversion exchange of information. I wear contacts, but I thought I'd give my eyes a rest tonight. Why? Do you mind?"

She danced ahead of him in the hallway, walking backward as she looked at him. "Yes, I think I do mind. You're still gorgeous. Can we maybe attach a fake nose and mustache to those glasses?"

"And I could blacken out my two front teeth?" Colin asked her as he jabbed the button to call the elevator. "You know, I've never had this problem before. Women—other women, not you—have always appreciated my looks."

"Oh, I do, I do," Holly assured him, then watched, smiling almost generously, as the doors to the elevator opened and a middle-aged woman all but stumbled flat on her face exiting the car, her attention all on Colin.

They stepped inside, the doors closed and Holly exploded into giggles. "Did you see that? That poor woman. You're a traffic hazard, Colin. Even in glasses."

"Does it count that I winked at her?" he asked, leaning against the side of the elevator car.

"You…you *winked* at her? Why?"

"To drive you crazy, why else?" he answered, then grabbed her hand in his as the doors opened once more, led her through the hotel foyer and through the exit that led directly onto the boardwalk.

The sun had already moved across the sky far enough

that the buildings lining the land-side of the boardwalk blocked some of its brightness, although Holly still wished she'd grabbed her sunglasses, because she'd rather Colin couldn't see the expression in her eyes.

"You enjoy it, don't you? Oh, you say you don't see what the fuss is all about, but you enjoy it. Women goggling at you, tripping over themselves. I mean, it's not that women are idiots, because we're not. But we're used to seeing really, *really* handsome men on screen, posing in magazines. Not walking out of an elevator in Ocean City, New Jersey. You're a shock to the system. Max is the same way. He doesn't just walk into a room, he *dominates* everyone in it, just by showing up."

"Max is in a whole other league, Holly. Max *is* Majestic Enterprises. I'm—" he pulled her close, grinned at her "—well, I'm just another pretty face. Although, if this face of mine is going to keep bothering you, come between us, I could maybe try to break my nose or something?"

"Don't be silly," she said, embarrassed. "I like your face. I'm crazy about your face. I—oh, hell, let's find something to eat so I can put something other than my foot in my mouth."

"Here we go," he said after they'd walked another long block, gulls laughing overhead, the incoming tide creeping up the sandy beach on the water-side of the raised boardwalk. "My old stomping grounds. Hey, Giovanni! Remember me?"

A rather large—and definitely *wide*—man dressed all in white, wearing a paper chef's hat and a stained white apron, looked up from his current job of ladling pizza sauce onto an uncooked crust. "Colin!" he exclaimed, wiping off his hands on his apron as he walked up to the wide counter separating the boardwalk from his pizza shop. He narrowed his eyes and glared at Colin. "You still owe me ten bucks for that pizza cutter you broke."

"Hey," Colin said, shaking the older man's hand, "I was trying to unstick that junk drawer of yours for you, remember? I'll bet you never did get it open."

Giovanni shrugged eloquently. "The drawer remains one of life's little mysteries. Another is where you've been all these years. And who is this lovely lady with you?"

Colin did the introductions, then asked if they could have one of Giovanni's special pizzas.

"Sure, and you can make it, just the way you like it. Come on, come on," he said, motioning for Colin to go around the L-shaped bar and enter the cramped work area. "And you, Miss Holly. You sit right here and watch the boy work. We'll see if he remembers, or if he's soon going to be wearing dough all over his face."

Colin laughed as he grabbed an apron from a shelf under the large worktable, then washed his hands in a stainless-steel sink fitted under the serving bar. "Ten bucks says I haven't forgotten a thing you taught me, Giovanni."

Holly climbed up on one of the green, imitation leather stools, and rested her chin in her hands. She looked at Colin, who now wore a paper chef's hat just like Giovanni's, and tried not to laugh. He looked *so* adorable. "Okay, Chef Colin," she goaded him, "do your magic for us. Pretend I'm sixteen, and just *drool-*

ing over the handsome pizza tosser. Unless that makes you nervous?''

"Nervous, him?" Giovanni said, sliding a wooden paddle beneath the pizza he'd just made, then slipping it into the brick oven. "He was my best, the best. If I had fifty cents for every slice of pizza those young girls bought—wait! I *do!*" And then he laughed, his round belly jiggling.

Holly smiled at the man, then watched Colin as he selected a softball-size ball of dough from a large plastic bowl on the worktable. He dusted the wooden table with flour, dusted his hands and forearms as well, then pounded on the ball of dough, flattening it until it was a thick, six-inch-round disk.

"Kind of small, don't you think?" she teased him as Giovanni placed a large paper cup of soda in front of her.

"Ah, but I have not yet begun to toss," Colin said, winking at her. He picked up the dough, eyed it for a moment. The next thing Holly knew, the fat disk was in the air, and growing wider, thinner.

Up went the dough, spinning in the air. Down came the dough, Colin deftly catching it, spinning it, lofting it into the air once more. The dough stayed in a re-markably proportioned circle, the inside of the circle growing thinner, the edges remaining thick.

One more toss and Colin flopped the dough onto the table. *Bam!* A ladle of sauce, deftly spread to cover every bit of dough except that thicker crust. *Bam!* Spices sprinkled from a large shaker. *Bam!* Two hand-fuls of cheese spread on the sauce. *Bam!* The wooden paddle slipped under the dough, the pizza transferred to the brick oven. *Bam!* Giovanni's now fully cooked pizza placed on a round metal tray Colin spun as he ran the sharp blade of a pizza cutter through it as his former boss waited on other customers.

"Well, I'm impressed," Holly admitted as Colin went back to the sink, washed his hands and forearms, grinned at her as he wiped himself dry on his apron. "Does Max know about this talent of yours? He might be misusing you as a hotshot executive. I mean, anybody can be an executive, but only a few talented people can make that kind of magic with pizza dough."

"You may laugh, but I'm feeling pretty proud of myself. Or maybe I shouldn't tell you that I worried I was going to lose control of that dough, and end up with it landing on the top of my head. Now hang on. I'll get us napkins, get myself a drink, and by then the pizza will be ready."

"Okay," Holly said around a mouthful of pizza a few minutes later, "now I'm *really* impressed. This is good!"

"Giovanni's secret pizza sauce," Colin told her. "It makes all the difference in the world."

"Is he open to bribes? Because, if I had this recipe, I could go into business for myself back in Allentown, and make a fortune."

"And I could toss the dough?"

Holly wiped some sauce off his chin with her napkin. "If you were in the window, tossing the dough, I wouldn't need Giovanni's secret recipe. Do you want that last slice? Because if you don't grab it in the next two seconds, it's mine."

Chapter Nine

They visited with Giovanni for another half hour, Colin catching up on news of the shop owner's wife and children, he and Holly admiring pictures of the man's grandchildren. And then they said good-night, promised to come back tomorrow, and headed off up the boardwalk once more.

The sun had completely slipped behind the buildings, and the breeze off the ocean had Holly shivering slightly as the wind ruffled the skirt of her sundress, nipped slightly at her bare shoulders.

Colin put his arm around her, drew her against his side, his strength, his warmth. "Come on, I'll buy you a sweatshirt," he said, directing her steps toward one of the many specialty shops along the boardwalk.

Holly thought about protesting, then remembered that she hadn't brought her wallet with her. She entered the shop, and went directly to an oversize sweatshirt that said He's With Me on it. "I like this one," she said.

"So do I," Colin agreed, and Holly felt her cheeks grow hot. "Is there a She's With Me to match it?"

"That's silly. The whole idea is silly," Holly told him, wishing she'd thought before she'd spoken. "I'm not all that into staking public claims."

"I am," Colin said, kissing the tip of her nose. "But you're probably right. Look, here's a cardigan-style sweatshirt. Simple yellow, small embroidered Ocean City logo on the pocket. Probably a better choice."

"Definitely," Holly agreed, relieved. "And I'll pay you back."

"Should I start running a tab?" he asked as they returned to the boardwalk, heading back to the hotel. "Just how platonic is this little exercise going to be?"

"Don't make fun of me, please," Holly said, pulling herself free from his grasp. "I'm having a very difficult time with this. Nobody ever proposed to me within twenty-four hours of meeting me before. I've been thrown a little off center. And then Julia horned in, Max, my own mother. This is all just happening too fast. You really don't even know me."

"Sure I do."

"No, you don't, Colin. Just like I know nothing about you. And I'm not so shallow that I'd let myself fall in love with a pretty face."

"I am," he said, surprising her. "I think I fell in love with you the moment I saw you. And you've got a very pretty face. Have I mentioned yet that your eyes sort of *crossed* when you were trying to tie my bow tie? Just adorable. I was a goner from that moment, I think."

"You're impossible!" Holly exclaimed, even as her heart began to sing. He'd said those little words: love you. He'd actually said them—at least two out of three of them. "Oh, all right," she added, sighing. "I'm not going to deny that I felt…*something,* when I first saw you. But I wouldn't call it love. That just doesn't happen in real life."

"It happened to your parents," Colin pointed out rationally, or irrationally, as Holly wanted to believe. "Why can't it have happened to us?"

"Because I don't *believe* in love at first sight, that's why. I would never trust myself enough to take such a giant leap after just *looking* at someone. So this can't be love, even if it feels like it. It's just—"

And then she stopped, blinked, looked up at Colin. "What did I just say?"

"I think you just said you don't trust yourself," Colin told her as they turned into the walkway leading back to the hotel. "I might also think you just said you definitely felt something more than animal attraction, or whatever you want to call it, for me. When we first met, when I kissed you on that runway, while we were together that first night. I think you felt something Holly, and I think you've been fighting it, and me, ever since."

"I have not."

"Really?" he asked, raising his eyebrows. "Let's investigate that a little, okay? First it was you didn't date male models. You were very emphatic about that. Then it was that I was too handsome. Now it's that you don't know me, and you refuse to make snap decisions. The longer the list gets, Holly, the less I believe any of it."

She felt flustered, confused, so she went on the attack as they rode up in the elevator. "I still don't know anything about you."

"Sure you do. You know I'm Max's cousin, you know how I grew up, where I work. You know I worked my way through college, so I'm not just a spoiled rich kid. You know I like dogs, your mother—not in that order, of course. You know that I'm not at my best early in the morning, that we like the same movies and music, that I'm stubborn and don't give up easily. Oh, and that I wear maroon briefs. There have been plenty of marriages based on a lot less."

"I give up," Holly said, throwing up her hands. "I can't fight anymore, I really can't. Please, just say goodnight, and we'll start over in the morning, okay?"

"Okay," he said, his grin sort of crooked, his eyes warm, so that the idea of melting into his arms seemed to be the best idea she'd had in her entire life. "Good night, Holly," he said, then slowly drew her into his arms, kissed her.

Then kissed her again.

And again.

Her arms went up around his neck, held him close.

He stepped his body closer, slid one leg between hers. Kissed her again.

He skimmed his hands up her sides, onto her arms, gently eased her back. "Good night."

"Good night," she said, wondering if that low, rather shaky voice was really her own.

She leaned against the door, watching as he walked down the hallway, longing to call him back, knowing she'd be out of her mind to call him back. But it hurt, it actually *hurt* to watch him walk away.

He stopped. Turned. Reached into his pocket. "Your

room key,'' he said, heading toward her once more, holding the key card in his hand.

"Thank you," Holly said, taking the card from him, then just standing there. Looking at him. While he looked at her. "Well, good night again."

"Yeah," he said, and his voice sounded a little strange, too. "Good night again."

She still just stood there, holding that damn key card.

Colin cupped her chin and cheek in his hand, leaned forward to kiss her once more. Again, she melted against him. Once more, his hands skimmed her sides, this time lingering just below her breasts, as if awaiting permission to touch her.

She moved against him, bit on his full bottom lip. Moaned softly as he moved his hands slightly higher, but not high enough. What did she have to do? Draw the man a diagram?

His mouth left hers, and he trailed kisses across her cheeks, down the length of her throat as she stood on tiptoe, trying to get closer, closer.

"Separate rooms," he breathed into her ear. "You promised your mother, remember?"

"Huh?" Holly said, blinking. Then she stepped back, shook herself, tried to concentrate on something other than the way she felt, the way he held her, the way he kissed her. "Oh, right. We really should say goodnight."

"Say it and mean it," Colin added, his grin not quite reaching his eyes for the very first time in her memory. "So, good night again." He kissed the tip of her nose. "Sleep tight." He kissed her mouth. "Don't let the bedbugs bite." He kissed her again.

And again. And again.

They were going everywhere and nowhere at the same time. Necking like teenagers who knew the porch light could come on at any moment. Not going too far, because anything more than kisses, caresses, would take both of them past the point of being able to stop, walk away.

Twice more he left her, never getting as far as the turn in the hallway, leading to the elevators. Twice more he came back, kissed her again. Held her. Pressed her head against his chest so that she could feel the ragged rise and fall of his chest, give her time to try to regulate her own breathing.

"This is nuts, crazy," he said, sliding his fingers through her hair, pressing his lips against her bare shoulder. "I've got to let you go."

"I know," Holly agreed. "I've got to let you go, too. This is just making everything more complicated."

"Maybe, but it's a pretty enjoyable complication, don't you think?" he asked her, and this time his smile did light in his eyes.

"Say good night, Colin," she told him, turning away, slipping the key card into the slot in the door. "And, this time, you're going to have to mean it. We both are." The lock clicked, the light on the lock turned green and she opened the door. "There. Good night."

"Sweet dreams," Colin whispered, his mouth against her ear.

"Now cut that out!" she protested, rubbing at her ear, that tingled. Just as her lips were tingling. Just as her entire body was tingling, singing.

"Yes, ma'am," he said, then turned on his heels, his

hands shoved in the pockets of his jeans, and walked away. She could hear him whistling as he turned the corner, went out of sight.

Holly closed the door behind her and all but collapsed against it. "I thought he'd never leave," she told herself, knowing that what she had really meant was: "I wish he'd never gone."

"So, cuz, how go the wars?"

"Hi, Max." Colin didn't even bother taking time to ask how Max how tracked him down at the Ocean City hotel. "Quite well, actually, if by quite well I mean she's still here and seems to be getting used to me."

"Used to you? That doesn't sound very romantic, Colin. Remember, you're a Rafferty. We have certain standards."

"And several drawbacks, I'm afraid, at least as far as Holly is concerned."

Max laughed. "Our good looks. Max Deuce has them, too, mostly thanks to his beautiful mother, I think, but then I'm rather prejudiced. Although I've never thought of the Rafferty looks as a liability."

"Maybe that's because you didn't have to compete with the bad impression made by Richard the Lousehearted," Colin said, pacing in his room, already wishing he'd gotten his act together sooner, and missed Max's call. "Good looks, for Holly, seem to mean shallow emotions."

"Richard's history," Max told him. "And Holly was never all that serious about him. She's only fighting you because she's falling so fast, so hard. She's looking for things that would turn her off and, not finding any, she's trying to convince herself what she feels for you is no more than physical attraction.''

Colin moved the phone away from his ear, looked at it, then drew it back, saying, ''Are you sure you're Max? Because you sound a lot like Julia.''

''Maybe that's because I just read you that last bit from a note my darling wife just passed to me. Look, Colin, you handle this the way you want to handle it, okay? If you want to stay in the States for a while longer, fine. Anything you want. Because Julia might be happy to see her best friend falling in love, but I'm doing handsprings over the idea of *you* falling in love.''

''So glad we're making the two of you so happy,'' Colin said, slipping his feet into his sneakers, bending to tie the laces.

''Oh, you are, you are. Wait, Julia's scribbling again. Oh hell, here—talk to her.''

''Colin?''

''Good morning, Julia,'' Colin answered, sitting down on the edge of the bed. ''What can I do for you? Maybe rent a video camera and put my entire courtship on tape? Anything I can do to entertain you, Julia.''

''My, we are testy in the morning, aren't we? And here I thought you and Holly were so compatible. Maybe I should warn you. She's one of those bright and sunny morning people, you know.''

''I—no, I didn't know that,'' Colin corrected quickly, knowing that anything else he might say would have Julia running even more questions by him, expecting detailed answers. ''Look, Julia, I really appreciate the call. I do. But Holly and I are doing really well. Honestly. We played some miniature golf yesterday, drove up to Atlantic City last night for a few hours. We've talked until we're just about hoarse. Except for horror movies—she likes them, I don't—we're about as compatible as two people can be.''

"And you're in love with her.'' It wasn't a question, it was a statement.

"And I'm in love with her,'' Colin repeated, smiling. "However, if you and Max don't mind, I think I'll do my own proposing, okay? Not that I don't appreciate all your help, because I do.''

"I can do more,'' Julia said, her voice low, rather mysterious.

Colin shook his head, then said no. "Really, Julia. No. We're heading back to Allentown tomorrow, I fly back to Paris on Friday. Between now and then, I'll figure out a way to propose. One that's better than just telling her I'm going to marry her as I hand her a hot dog.''

"Well, I should hope so, Colin,'' Julia told him, laughing. "But, you see, the thing is, I had this idea. Now, just because I had this idea doesn't mean *you* have to like it, but it's such a *good* idea, and Irene agrees, and Max—well, you know Max. He likes anything if he can be in on it. May I at least tell you about it?''

Colin made a face, then gave in to the inevitable. "Sure, Julia. Tell me about it.'' He stayed on the edge of the bed, listening, nodding his head, listening some more…smiling.

Holly planted both feet on the boardwalk, refusing to move. "No. I can't do that. It's silly.''

She and Colin had spent another wonderful day together. An early breakfast, a walk on the beach. They'd spent two hours browsing through a used book store, agreeing on authors they liked, suggesting authors the other hadn't read. Colin had purchased three Stephen King books Holly recommended to him, and she'd somehow gotten talked into giving *War and Peace* another try after tossing the book across the room when it had been one of her choices to read for a high school Literature class.

But volleyball? She didn't play volleyball.

"I don't know the rules," she told Colin as he took her hand, led her toward the steps down to the beach. "Besides, maybe they have enough players," she added, looking at the group of teenagers, both boys and girls, gathering on the sand.

Just then a blond teen with muscles bulging everywhere trotted across the sand and called out, "You wanna play? We're just horsing around."

"Can you use two more?" Colin called back to him.

"One more, one more," Holly yelled, cupping her hands around her mouth. "He means *one* more."

"Chicken," Colin teased.

A red flag immediately went up inside Holly's head. Chicken? He dared to call her *chicken?* "You're on," she declared, kicking off her sandals, feeling the coolness of the afternoon sand, still wet from high tide. "Where do you want me?" she asked the blonde, who pointed to the far side of the net.

"Great," Holly said, joining the teens who would make up her team, half boys, half girls. She zeroed in on a smiling brunette with shiny teeth braces. "Okay, quick course on the rules. Where do I stand, what do I do?"

What she did was eat sand. Lots of it. But each time she pushed herself up to her knees again, stood up again, brushed herself off again, she narrowed her eyes, faced the net and tried again.

Colin, of course, was brilliant. He served for his team, then moved closer to the net, leaping high in the air to slam the volleyball back at Holly's team, scoring point after point.

Not that her team was a bunch of slackers. For each point Colin's team scored, Holly's team came back with a point of their own, until the brunette motioned for Holly to come over to her so she could explain: "Tie-breaker. We score now or it's all over, okay? Your turn to serve."

Holly's stomach dropped to her toes. "*My* turn to serve? But you saw what I did last time. I couldn't even get it over the net."

"That's because you slapped at it," the teen told her. "Make a fist. Hit it with your fist. Uppercut it. Like this. See? Come on, you can do it."

Feeling very much like the little engine that *couldn't*, Holly retreated to her spot, held the volleyball in both hands, wishing she could disappear.

And then she heard it. Colin's voice. "Game's in the bag now, team!" he called out, looking straight at her. Grinning straight at her.

"Oh, challenging me again, are you?" Holly whispered, glaring back at him. "Trying to make me mad, make me screw up. Well, Holly Hollis doesn't screw up, buster!"

She tossed the volleyball into the air, then slammed it with her fist—and part of her forearm, but who cared about style at a time like this? The ball sailed over the net, straight at Colin, who deftly sent it back into the air so a teammate could try slamming it over the net, into the sand.

Except his teammate was so busy planning his part of the victory celebration that he miss-hit the ball and it clipped the net, fell back, landed at Colin's feet.

Holly's team jumped and yelled and generally carried on like the winners they were, all while Holly stood quietly, watching Colin as he shook hands with everyone, then walked toward her.

"You did that on purpose," she accused him, her eyelids narrowed. "You purposely said that about me so that I'd get mad, knowing that I'd get so mad I'd hit the ball with everything that was in me. Didn't you?"

"Who? Me? Now why would I do that?" Colin asked, waving at the teens as he led Holly back to the place where they'd kicked off their footwear.

"You'd do it because you know me so well. And I'm beginning to think I don't like that you know me so well. What am I? Some sort of Pavlov's dog? Reacting to stimulus? It's insulting."

Colin stood still as Holly braced herself against him, slid into her sandals. "Holly, we all react to stimulus."

"No, we don't."

"Sure we do. For instance," he said, then swooped down on her, caught her mouth with his own. His arms slid around her waist, holding her tight, and she could taste sand and salt on his lips. Her arms went up and over his shoulders, holding him tight because there was nothing in the world she could ever want more than to hold him, hold him tight.

In the distance, the teenagers hooted and applauded, called out encouragement.

"See?" Colin said, moving slightly back, so that his smiling mouth was now inches from hers. "You look at me, your eyes flashing emerald fire. Stimulus. I kiss you. Reaction to stimulus. I can't help myself. I don't *want* to help myself."

Holly tried to think, but it was difficult. She was much too involved in holding him, being held, watching his mouth move as he spoke, wishing that mouth on hers once more. "Yes, well...that is, I...oh!" She dropped her arms, headed for the steps leading up to the boardwalk "You're impossible!"

"I'm getting to you, aren't I?" he asked, tagging after her, catching up to her and slipping his arm around her waist.

"You are *not* getting to me," she told him, wishing she sounded more convincing. "I didn't want this. I didn't want *any* of this."

He stopped, drew her to a halt as well. "You didn't want any of what, Holly?"

She sighed, spread her arms. "*This*. Ninety-five percent of the world might be looking for love and all of that, but I'm not."

"Neither was I," Colin told her, brushing some dried sand from her cheek. "That's something else we have in common. We're in that five percent bracket."

"Very funny," Holly growled, then jammed both hands on her hips. "Look. I wasn't looking for you, you just showed up. You weren't looking for me, I just happened to be there. And we felt this…this *thing* happening that neither of us expected.''

''Our mutual crush,'' Colin said, nodding his head. ''Yes, I remember. Do you still think that's all it is?''

Holly looked down at her sand-dusted toes. ''I don't know.'' Then she looked up at him, tears stinging her eyes. ''I've…well, there was Richard…but that was just dumb and I couldn't possibly compare what I thought I felt for him with what I…but this is happening so *fast,* you know? I thought…hey, a couple of days and this would all go away…''

''But it hasn't, has it?'' Colin asked her, taking a handkerchief from his back pocket and wiping at her wet cheeks. ''And it's scaring the hell out of you. Why?''

''I don't know,'' Holly answered honestly. ''I just don't know. Maybe…maybe I'm afraid I don't know what makes a good relationship. What makes it last, that is.''

''Love, Holly,'' Colin said, taking her hand, heading toward their hotel. ''Love makes a relationship last. It might not be a very original answer, but it's all I've got to offer. But if you need more time, then that's what you'll have. I promise, no more bum's rush, okay? I leave for Paris in two days. The next move is up to you.''

''Oh, Colin,'' Holly said, sighed. ''Let's go home. Horrified as I am to even say this, I think I want to talk to my mother.''

Holly squeezed her eyes shut, tried to think. What on earth was she doing? How had she let Julia talk her into this? Had she been in this much of a daze since return-ing from the shore?

She kept her eyes closed, remembered the long trip back from Ocean City. Well, the first half of the trip had been long…and silent…and definitely uncomfort-able. But then Colin had tuned the radio to an oldies' station. He'd begun humming along with one song, then began singing along with the next one, until Holly had no choice but to join in.

"Your grandfather was right," he'd said to her after that first song was over. "You *are* loud."

"But not very good," she'd complained.

"I think you're great. And our voices sound pretty good together. Oh—listen. Do you know the words to this one?"

She had, and they'd sung together to the song, and to every song, all the rest of the way home. Then he'd carried her suitcases into the apartment, kissed her on the cheek and left her standing there. He hadn't said he'd call, he hadn't said goodbye. He'd just kissed her, then walked away.

Which was why, Holly told herself, she had come into work this morning, Friday morning, the day Colin would fly back to Paris.

Without saying goodbye.

She was so angry with him! What was he trying to prove now? That absence made the heart grow fonder? After the two of them had been together every day, was he trying to prove that she'd miss him when he was gone? Was he trying to get her to recognize what he said he already knew—that there was such a thing as love at first sight? That their mutual crush was so much more than just a crush, some intense physical attraction?

If so, he was certainly proving his point. She hadn't slept all night. She hadn't eaten. She certainly hadn't smiled. She hadn't even had the energy to think up an excuse that would convince Julia that she wasn't in the mood to play model for the first petite gown Julia had dreamed up for the bridal line.

So here she was, standing on the platform in the fitting room, wearing the finished product that had been only a sketch a few days earlier.

Julia and Irene had dressed her, then fussed over her, trying on different veils, Julia pinning the netting to different headpieces until she found the one she liked best with the gown.

"Gorgeous," Irene had declared at last, standing behind Holly, fluffing out the cathedral train, arranging the long veil over it. "Absolutely gorgeous. Just perfect for the petite figure, Julia."

"Holly?" Julia had asked as she checked the time on her wristwatch. "How do you feel? You don't feel overwhelmed, do you?"

"Emotionally or physically?" Holly had grumbled under her breath, looking at her reflection, feeling all the sadness of the world pressing down on her bare shoulders. "I feel fine, Julia," she then said more loudly. "This is the way it should be. Every bride should be able to try on a gown at least close to her own size, so she can get an idea how the finished product will look on her. You did good, Julia. Now, can I please get out of this thing? It's starting to itch."

Which had been entirely the wrong thing to say, because Julia had immediately asked *where* it itched, and had then taken the gown away for some quick adjustments to the lining, telling Holly to stay where she was so they could try the gown again once it was fixed.

Which had left Holly standing on the platform in a long-line bra, two huge net petticoats still snapped around her slim waist. "Now there's a look," she'd said to Irene, who had teasingly replaced the veil on Holly's head. "Why the veil, Irene?"

"Oh, I don't know. It just seemed easier to put it back on you than to hang it up. Julia's sure to want to see the whole effect one more time. Holly, do you have the time?"

Holly glanced at her wrist. "Eleven-thirty. Julia keeps checking the time, too. What's going on? Are we expecting an important call? You seem a little strung-out, Irene, a little nervous."

"I'm never nervous, dear," Irene said, and lifted her chin as she brushed back through the curtain, out of sight, only to return scant seconds later, wearing the strangest smile on her face. "Holly? Your mother's here."

Holly looked at her watch again, frowned. "Already? I told her I wouldn't be ready until noon." She lifted her shoulders, shrugged. "Okay. Would you please ask her to just come on back here? Thanks, Irene."

She winced involuntarily as she heard her mother's brisk footsteps approaching over the bare hardwood floor. Julia might be satisfied with the "whole effect," but her mother would be pulling out her tissues and calling Holly her "baby." She quickly reached up to lift the veil from her head.

"Holly! Oh, my! Oh, my goodness, *look* at you!"

Too late. "Hi, Mom. I'm just helping Julia out with the new petite-size gowns. What do you think of this one? The bustier look a little much?"

Hillary Hollis rolled her eyes, put her thin coat and her purse down on the wooden folding chair in the corner. "I was referring to the veil, dear. Do you think I don't know you're in your underwear? Nobody gets married in a bra and slip."

Holly grinned. "Obviously you haven't seen some of the gowns out there these days, Mom." And then she sobered. "Mom. Could I ask you a question?"

"Of course, sweetheart," Hillary said, fussing with the folds in the veil. "I may not have the answer, but I'll certainly do my best."

"You always do your best, Mom," Holly told her quietly, her heart bursting with love for this woman who managed all of her family so effortlessly, made them all feel so special, so loved. So loved. And that brought her back to her question. "Mom, how did you know you were in love with Dad? I mean, that you were *really* in love with him? This is important, Mom. Probably the most important question I'll ever ask."

Holly watched as her mother's eyes—green, just like hers—went rather soft and dreamy. All these years, all the trials and arguments and minor tragedies, and her mother's eyes still went soft and dreamy when she thought about being in love with her Howard. Amazing. And something to wish she had for herself. "Mom?" she prompted.

Hillary sighed. "Well, darling, I wish I had an easy answer for you, but I don't. There are the symptoms, of course. Can't eat, can't sleep, can't think of anything but him—that sort of thing. But *knowing* that you're in love? I don't think that's something we *know,* not right away. We *believe.* Yes, that's it. We *believe* we're in love, and then we take that next step, a real leap of faith, *hoping* that what we have, what we think we have, is the real thing."

"I don't understand," Holly said honestly.

"No, of course you don't," Hillary said, nodding. "We marry because we think we're in love, sweetheart. That's how every marriage starts. But *staying* in love takes real commitment, through the good times, through the bad times. I loved your father the moment I saw him, Holly, but I didn't really understand how *much* I loved him until we'd shared a few joys, weathered a few storms together. Love, the sort that lasts a lifetime, is really a gamble. We can't be one hundred percent sure, going into a marriage, that love will endure, grow. But if we love, we take that leap of faith. To do anything else, to deny what we feel? Well, why would anyone do that? Think what they might miss."

"No guarantees," Holly said on a sigh.

Hillary reached up, patted her daughter's cheek. "They're men, sweetheart, not cars. They don't come with warranties. Now tell me, do you love Colin? Because we are talking about Colin, aren't we?"

Holly bit her lips together, nodded. "We're talking about Colin. And, yes, I do love him. Or, at least, I know I've never felt this way before, not ever. And I'm feeling some of the stupidest things, Mom. I want to cook for him, I want to make a home for him. I want—dear, God, I want *babies*. I want to wake up in the morning and see his face with a morning beard. I want to sleep in his arms. I want to talk to him, tell him everything I've never said to another living soul—and I know he'd listen, he'd understand.''

She raised both hands to her cheeks. ''Oh, Mom, do you *hear* me. Did you ever think you'd hear me say anything like this?''

''Gown's ready,'' Julia said, holding the ivory organza creation high in front of her as she reentered the fitting room from the factory. ''Oh, hi, Hillary. I don't know where Irene went, so maybe you could help me with this? We were running a little ahead of schedule, but now we really should be ready.''

''Yes, I saw that as I came in,'' Hillary said as Holly looked at Julia suspiciously. ''It looks beautiful. I love organza.''

''Excuse me, but is there something I should know?'' Holly asked, only to be ignored, as if she were a mannequin, not a real, living person.

''Yes, but it's not quite right for Holly,'' Julia said once the veil had been removed, the gown slipped over Holly's head, and the veil once more in place. ''I had thought so, but it's not quite sophisticated enough. That's one of the problems with petite sizes. We tend to forget that all petites aren't either eighteen or eighty. I've tried to cover that lack in my ready-to-wear, and now I have to do it again with the bridal wear.''

''I like this one,'' Holly said, suddenly feeling quite possessive of the gown she wore. She slanted her head to the side. ''Of course, I do like *peau de soie,* and if there could be just a bit of Alencon lace? I know huge puffy sleeves would drown me, but is there any reason we couldn't modify the sleeves a little, cut them down to my size?''

Julia held up one finger. "I know just what you mean. December, right? Simplified, but still more dramatic, more sophisticated. Hillary? If you'd like, you could help me as I sketch the idea I'm getting. Holly, it doesn't itch anymore, does it? Good. Now, you just stay right here, and I'll send Irene in to help you out of that gown."

"Yes, but—" Holly began, then realized she was talking to empty space. "Great. Just what I need to do, stand around in a wedding gown all day. And what was all that business about the time?"

She stood, tapping one foot, thinking over everything her mother had said, marveling that she hadn't known just how brilliant her mother was. She'd always seen her as *mom,* not as a woman, and yet she felt closer to her right now than she had since she'd been a little girl.

She looked at her watch once more—having her own obsession with time today—and wondered where Colin was, if he'd already left his hotel in New York, was winging back to Paris, so graciously and maddeningly giving her the time and space she so stupidly thought she'd wanted, needed.

And she came to a decision. Two, actually. One: she was an idiot. Two: she didn't have to remain an idiot.

"Irene?" she called out. "Could you come in here and help me, please?" Reaching behind her, she tried to grab hold of the zipper, get herself out of the gown. She wanted to call the Waldorf, see if Colin had checked out yet. It was either that, or she was going to have to fly to Paris. Maybe she'd wait until he was biting down on a croissant at some outdoor trendy café on the West Bank, then tell him she was pretty sure she was going to marry him. Turnabout was, after all, fair play.

Just as her fingertips finally made contact with the zipper, Holly realized something else. It was quiet. Too quiet. The hum from the sewing machines was missing. Nobody was talking, laughing. The door to the office was closed, so she didn't hear any ringing phones, the beep of the fax. Not even the sometimes annoying play of the music system broke the silence.

Why? What was going on? Where had everyone gone?

And then the silence was broken as the music system came to life. She looked up at one of the speakers, as if an answer could be found, then felt the presence of somebody else in the fitting room. She turned, looked, saw everything and everyone she wanted to see.

"You're so beautiful."

"Colin?" Holly took a step forward, nearly tumbling off the platform. "What—what are you doing here? You're supposed to be flying to Paris. That's where I just decided to go, to be with you. And…and what are you wearing?"

"Those of us in the know call it a tux," he said, walking toward her, magnificent in his tuxedo, that whole Greek god come to life thing hitting her all over again, just as it had that first day.

He held out his hand, and she held hers out to him, let him help her down from the platform.

"I had this whole romantic speech planned, telling you how I can't live without you, about how much I love you, about how I worked it out with Max that after you and I honeymoon in Paris until Christmas, I'll be heading up the offices in New Jersey. All that good stuff,'' he said quietly as he looked at her, as he just kept looking at her. ''This was going to be my big proposal. As a matter of fact, I think I'm supposed to be down on one knee right now. It all seemed like such a great plan at the time. Everybody thought so. Except now I can't remember anything. I can only look at you.''

She caught her breath as she realized that his eyes were overbright. ''Colin?'' she asked, feeling tears stinging at her own eyes. ''Are you trying to ask me something?''

His smile was soft, and she felt herself melting toward him, so that she had to put a hand against his chest, to steady herself.

''I've *been* trying to ask you something, darling, from the moment we met. The rest of this was Julia's idea, her idea of a romantic proposal scene. Except the music. Irene supplied the music.''

Holly closed her eyes, listened. ''Frank Sinatra?''

''Irene's favorite. Miss Hollis, may I have this dance?'' He took in a deep breath, let it out slowly. ''May I have every dance, for the next hundred years?''

Holly blinked, nodded. Still looking just at him, seeing no one but him, she tugged at her train until she could fold its length over her arm, then stepped closer to Colin, stepped into his waiting arms.

Holly rested her head against his chest as he sang along with Ole Blue Eyes, sang the words to the second verse of what would become their own special song, would always be their own special song: "I've Got A Crush On You."

The curtain behind Holly split open at the middle, and Julia, Hillary, Irene, and even Max poked their heads into the room, all of them smiling, all of them believing that he or she had been successful cupids.

Colin saw everyone, mouthed a silent "thank you," and then pressed a kiss against Holly's temple. He drew her closer, and the two of them began to move to the music of their lives....

* * * * *

HARLEQUIN® *Romance*.

**From the Heart.
For the Heart.**

Get swept away into the Outback
with two of Harlequin Romance's
top authors.

Coming in December...

Claiming the Cattleman's Heart

BY BARBARA HANNAY

And in January don't miss...

Outback Man Seeks Wife

BY MARGARET WAY

REQUEST YOUR FREE BOOKS!
2 FREE NOVELS PLUS 2
FREE GIFTS!

HARLEQUIN ROMANCE®

From the Heart, For the Heart

YES! Please send me 2 FREE Harlequin Romance® novels and my 2 FREE gifts. After receiving them, if I don't wish to receive any more books, I can return the shipping statement marked "cancel." If I don't cancel, I will receive 4 brand-new novels every month and be billed just $3.57 per book in the U.S., or $4.05 per book in Canada, plus 25¢ shipping and handling per book and applicable taxes, if any*. That's a savings of over 15% off the cover price! I understand that accepting the 2 free books and gifts places me under no obligation to buy anything. I can always return a shipment and cancel at any time. Even if I never buy another book from Harlequin, the two free books and gifts are mine to keep forever.

114 HDN EEV7 314 HDN EEWK

Name	(PLEASE PRINT)

Address	Apt.

City	State/Prov.	Zip/Postal Code

Signature (if under 18, a parent or guardian must sign)

Mail to Harlequin Reader Service®:

IN U.S.A.	**IN CANADA**
P.O. Box 1867	P.O. Box 609
Buffalo, NY	Fort Erie, Ontario
14240-1867	L2A 5X3

Not valid to current Harlequin Romance subscribers.

Want to try two free books from another line?
Call 1-800-873-8635 or visit www.morefreebooks.com.

* Terms and prices subject to change without notice. NY residents add applicable sales tax. Canadian residents will be charged applicable provincial taxes and GST. This offer is limited to one order per household. All orders subject to approval. Credit or debit balances in a customer's account(s) may be offset by any other outstanding balance owed by or to the customer. Please allow 4 to 6 weeks for delivery.

HR06

Silhouette Desire

USA TODAY bestselling author

BARBARA McCAULEY

continues her award-winning series

SECRETS!

**A NEW BLACKHAWK FAMILY
HAS BEEN DISCOVERED...
AND THE SCANDALS ARE SET TO FLY!**

She touched him once and now
Alaina Blackhawk is certain horse rancher
DJ Bradshaw will be her first lover. But will
the millionaire Texan allow her to leave
once he makes her his own?

Blackhawk's Bond

On sale December 2006 (SD #1766)

Available at your favorite retail outlet.